ALL
Rogues
LEAD TO
RUIN

 THE GARDEN GIRLS

ALL ROGUES LEAD TO RUIN

BOOK ONE OF *THE GARDEN GIRLS* SERIES
JEMMA FROST

ALSO BY JEMMA FROST

Charming Dr. Forrester

Dedicated to all the dreamers out there. You've got this.

PROLOGUE

September 1870, Hampshire, England

"I'M LEAVING HAMPSHIRE."

Three pairs of eyes looked up in shock at their youngest sister, Hazel's, pronouncement — the cozy Sunday evening, previously filled with reading and embroidery, taking an unexpected turn.

"What do you mean you're leaving? Where exactly are you going?" The practical one of the bunch as the eldest, Caraway asked the foremost question on their minds.

Setting aside the letter she'd received earlier, Hazel stood before her sisters, prepared to defend her decision. Sweat tracked down her back, but she was determined in her course. "A while back, I wrote Papa's old friend, Mr. Kilney, about a position at his library in Manchester. He said he'd keep me in mind for any possible openings, though my mourning period would prevent him from hiring me prior to its end."

A fire crackled in the hearth, casting shadows over the perplexed faces of her sisters while Hazel waited for them to digest the information and understand the significance of their meaning.

"And our mourning officially ended last week..." Lily mused, arms crossed over her chest while trouser-clad legs mimicked the position. As the second youngest, she was the most spirited and preferred running around in trousers compared to skirts — a fact that the local villagers had long ago learned to accept from one of the eccentric Taylor girls, if not approve.

"Precisely. I sent him a missive last Wednesday to inquire about the status of available positions, and there's his reply." She pointed to the folded paper. Worn despite the letter's recent arrival, it bore the signs of constant fiddling as Hazel contemplated how to inform Caraway, Lily, and Iris of her upcoming departure from their childhood home. "He's looking for an extra hand around the library and is willing to hire me. Even going so far as to allow me to stay with him and his wife as part of my wages. I start the fifteenth."

"But that's less than a week away! And you can't move alone to a new city without a chaperone," Caraway said, beginning to pace around the small room, skirts swishing back and forth in agitation. The distress in her voice gave Hazel a moment of remorse for causing her family to worry yet again, but she couldn't stay in Hampshire any longer. Memories bombarded her everywhere.

The small desk for writing, the one that used to be her father's. The lush garden surrounding their cottage, a testament to her mother's favorite pastime. And worst of all, the now-repaired bridge that had broken a year ago as the carriage carrying Hazel and their parents crossed it, sending them tumbling into the dry, rocky creek below. The reminder she'd survived while their parents had not.

Hampshire had become a stifling mortuary to her past, and the need to escape itched beneath her skin.

"At three and twenty, I'm perfectly capable of taking care of myself. Besides, I'll be a guest of Mr. Kilney and his wife; if I'm ever in need of anything, they'll be available."

"But what about marriage?" Iris asked. Though technically their cousin, she'd been raised since a baby with the Taylors, so they were sisters in all but blood.

Hazel laughed and pointed out the window towards the village down the road. "Do you see any suitors clamoring for my attention? I'll have a better chance of securing a match in Manchester than here."

Though it's not on my agenda for the future.

Procuring a husband should be the height of her ambition—her life's only duty. But she wasn't ready for marriage and children, to be settled so securely before exploring the world. All her life had been spent in the country, and while idyllic, her family's humble cottage along with the neighboring village provided little interest for her adventurous spirit.

"Not if you're busy working all the time." Lily's sarcastic tone chafed, but Hazel ignored the barbed comment. For months, Lily had been acting strangely. Always the fiery tempest in their family, lately her angry outbursts had escalated. They'd all learned to leave her alone to deal with whatever was roiling around inside her or else get a verbal laceration.

"I'm not concerned with finding a husband anyway; I need to publish my book first. And working in a library will be the perfect writing setting." Full of ideas and enamored with creating new worlds, she'd decided to finally make her dream a reality. After all, if a carriage accident could nearly end her life, then she didn't have time to waste.

With so many stories floating around in her head, it had taken some willpower to sit down and sift through the pages of notes written over the years to find the one story that held the most merit. Finally, she'd found it: the journey of a fairy searching for a stolen family heirloom with the help of her woodland friends.

Writing provided an escape unmatched by any other pastime. Learning the usual skills expected of a lady had never been Hazel's strong suit, and she'd been fortunate to be raised by parents who encouraged such unique pursuits, echoing their own peculiar interests. With their loss never far from her mind, the desire to become a published author solidified into a fervent need — their deaths must not be in vain because she'd failed to accomplish anything notable with her second chance at life.

"You can't truly believe someone will want to publish a children's fantasy from a single woman with no connections or drop of blue blood," Lily scoffed, a brow of skepticism scrunching her forehead.

"Yes, I do, and they *will* after reading it. Just because you've never endeavored to want anything beyond Hampshire doesn't mean I'm willing to molder away in the country." Hazel glared at Lily in rebuttal. Fingers itching to wring sense into her sisters, she stuffed them in her skirts. She would not be discouraged. If these spoken doubts caused her to fold, what hope did Manchester hold where professional publishing houses resided?

"Why, you..." Lily jumped to her feet and took a step toward Hazel, but Caraway pushed between them — a normal occurrence when it came to her two siblings. Youth bred wild tempers and outspoken personalities in the youngest Taylor girls whereas Caraway and Iris held the reserve on calm, cool, and collected.

"Now, now...We're getting off course. Hazel, I admire your courage to take on such a venture, but the fact remains that I can't allow you to live alone in a city we've never even visited. That's an industrial town much different than what you're used to here. It wouldn't be safe or proper even with the Kilneys nearby."

"As difficult as it may be for you to hear this, Cara, I don't need your permission, and the matter is settled. I have my portion of what Papa left us, and I'll be taking the train next Monday bound for Manchester." Hazel straightened to her full height, mere inches above Caraway's short stature, her mouth set in a firm line as her blue gaze never wavered. "I'm sorry this comes as a shock, but it's happening despite what any of you say."

Stern declaration resounding in the stunned silence, she swept out of the cottage to the gardens since an ambush in their shared bedroom above the main floor didn't appeal.

I'll show them. I'll prove them wrong.

Moonlight scattered on the petals of her mother's roses as a light chill brushed over her exposed arms; she should have grabbed a shawl in the midst of her exit. Soon the frost would arrive as autumn faded into winter, and much of the garden would lay dormant until spring. But she planned on blooming earlier — to be one of those new seedlings, sprouting, spreading their tendrils towards the sun despite the season.

This time next week, the life she'd dreamed of would begin. The days would be filled with organizing and shelving books in the library, exploring the different realms opened to her while at night, she'd write and draw the illustrations for her children's book.

But most importantly, Hazel would avoid any signs of her past life — tokens cementing the niggling thought that their parents should still be alive — not her.

CHAPTER ONE

October 1870, Manchester, England

FOG CLUNG TO JONATHAN Travers, turning his skin clammy to match the ball of nerves rolling around his belly, as he rapped a fist on the wooden door of his mark. Something felt off. It was unnaturally quiet on the lonely street, despite the late hour, as if the entire block held its breath, waiting.

And when these premonitions of danger slithered through Jonathan's mind, they were usually right. Motioning for his partner, Max, to back away into the dim cobblestoned street, a deep breath filled his lungs and he prepared himself for what they'd find inside the dark flat.

Let me be wrong.

For once, he'd like an easy night but knew it was too much to ask in his line of work: debt collector for the notorious Cobblewallers Gang. A title he used to wear proudly, strutting through Devil's Haven like a damn peacock, enjoying the fear and respect the association with such a dangerous group wrought.

And a job like tonight? It would have sent anticipation running down his spine, causing his blood to pump in eagerness.

But no longer.

Not after inheriting his younger brother, Pete, as a ward when their parents died. Not after seeing what pride and selfishness got him. *Nothing good, that's for damn sure. Now, focus.*

Kicking the door open, Jonathan and Max barged into the empty room, though the tang of fear hung heavy in the air. They weren't alone.

Andrew Jasper had fallen behind on his payments to the Cobblewallers Gang after racking up a sizable debt, so it was time for their particular brand of persuasion. Jonathan only hoped Jasper would listen to reason instead of needing to resort to Max's physical punishments.

"It's no use hiding. Lucien wants his money, and we're here to collect," Jonathan said as they searched the flat. Sparse and dirty, there weren't many places for a man to hide, yet there was no sign of Jasper.

At least he lives alone.

And Jonathan thanked God they wouldn't have to deal with family witnesses. Those were the worst nights.

Heading towards a closet, he rifled through worn clothing, pressing carefully on the walls for any secret doors and finding none to his consternation. *Where the hell are you?* Jonathan started to walk away when a fortuitous creaking sounded below him. He glanced at Max before kneeling down to trace the floorboards until a loose one wiggled under the pressure. Prying it up, he could just make out the gleam of a pistol before jerking to the side as a blast echoed in the room.

"Bloody hell!" Rolling to his feet, Jonathan retreated from the opening, calling out, "That wasn't very smart, Jasper. You can't stay down there forever, sooner or later you'll run out of bullets. Why don't you make things easier on yourself and come on up?" He forced a cajoling note into his voice when all he really wanted to do was wring the man's neck, but he rarely participated in the violent part of their meetings these days. Instead, he provided the charming persuasion while Max followed up with the force of his fists when needed.

Though Jonathan would make an exception today; something about almost getting his head blown off.

"Go away! I don't have his money!"

"Now, we know that's not true. Bart Thompson saw you exiting Lewiston's shop yesterday after unloading a couple of baubles. Just give us something to show your good faith, and we'll extend your deadline until next week. We're not unreasonable."

Max snorted, knowing full well such an offer only served to dig Jasper deeper into a hole with more interest heaped on top of his already enormous debt. But that would be a problem for next week if the man cooperated tonight.

A never-ending cycle. Jonathan inwardly sighed.

"You think I'll trust the word of one of Lucien's henchmen? Piss off!" Another warning shot rang out. *That's two.* By Jonathan's estimation, the man probably only had four shots left before needing to reload.

"Afraid we can't do that," Jonathan said as he studied the room to find a way to subdue Jasper. A set of matches on a table sparked an idea.

Rolling up some loose sheets of paper, he struck a match and lit the bundle before tossing it into the hole. Jasper yelped and Jonathan took advantage of his distraction by hopping into the cramped hiding spot and wrestling the gun away, their scuffling feet stomping out the tiny blaze.

He added a punch to the man's jaw for good measure then tucked the pistol into his waistband and raised Jasper's arms for Max to grab hold before climbing out himself. Max wasted no time tying the groaning man to a spindly chair with a length of rope they kept handy for such circumstances.

A blanket of weariness settled on Jonathan's shoulders at the familiar tableau as the energy from the brief tussle faded away. Someday, he wouldn't have to dodge bullets or intimidate gutter scum to collect debts for the king sewer rat himself, Amos Lucien, head of the Cobblewallers Gang.

But it's not tonight.

Cracking the knuckles on his fist, Jonathan strode forward to complete their business now that Jasper was restrained. A quarter-hour later, they left the man with a bloody nose and a partial payment jangled in a pouch tucked inside Jonathan's jacket.

"Bloody fool," Max muttered, and Jonathan couldn't agree more as they traipsed through the rookery to their next stop. Unfortunately, the night progressed with much the same — fools abounding at every turn. No one seemed amenable to his entreaties, so it was a night of violence all around.

When dawn lightened the sky, they returned to Lucien's den to drop off the collected money before going their separate ways. Max knocked twice on a barred door that opened to let them in before slamming shut again. Vignettes of people sat around the gambling den: one table for vingt-et-un, another for craps. And in the murky corners of the smoky room, men lounged with heavily made-up women, the prostitutes Lucien pimped out on the side.

Ignoring the spectacle, both men walked back to Lucien's office where he hunched over a large book, no doubt the accounts for every poor Tom, Dick, and Harry who owed him. They didn't always see Lucien — only when they'd collected a certain amount and he was curious about their dealings.

"Gentlemen, welcome. And how did we fare this fine evening?" Lucien leaned back in his leather chair, a squeaking sound coming from the weight of such a move. Lacing sausage fingers over a rotund stomach, he eyed Jonathan; it was his job to report.

"Justin Morrissey is paid in full. Timothy Kenton..." By rote, he recited the list of names and sums, skipping over mentioning the altercations as they were a routine part of the job.

"Good work, boys. How about a drink? I've got your favorite whiskey, Jonny." He hated that nickname. It made him feel like the gawky boy of his early days spent with the Cobblewallers, back when he idolized Lucien and dreamed of becoming just like him.

Youthful ignorance.

"I'm afraid I must decline. Pete will be awake soon, and I need to get home."

"Listen to you." Lucien chortled. "You sound like a nursemaid tending to her charge."

Gritting his teeth at the comparison, Jonathan plastered on a pleasant expression before dipping his head in a cursory farewell. "Perhaps, but I take my responsibilities seriously. You should appreciate such a trait."

Lucien scoffed, waving them off, and Jonathan's tense shoulders marginally relaxed as he swept out of the room, Max following closely behind until they reached the alley. A quick good-bye echoed from him before he disappeared into the shadows, and Jonathan was finally alone.

Stuffing chilled hands into his pockets, he hurried home — to a cold bed and battering thoughts of Jonathan's mistakes. A chain of metal links weighed around his ankles, all forged by his past choices and anchoring him to this world of greed and violence with little hope of escaping.

But I'm working on improving my odds.

Plans for a better future lay before him — a broken and obstacle-filled track, but one he was determined to conquer if not for himself than for Pete. With that in mind, he turned his attention towards next steps instead of the reality of his current circumstances.

SHE'S BACK AGAIN.

Jonathan watched as the pretty little blonde made her way to the cracked fountain at the center of Devil's Haven where children waited for her arrival, ready to hear the day's passage.

A week ago, he'd been heading home, eager to sleep after an extended night of work, when he'd seen the woman reading a book to the group. With the passing of the Forster Law recently, schools had cropped up all over England though the people of Devil's Haven were still wary of such a place and even more concerned about losing a part of their household's income to a child turned student. Not that many could pay the tuition even for the rudimentary school a few blocks away.

Thus, the gathered children were a mix of a few lucky ones on lunch break and those too young to work but too poor to attend classes.

For his part, he appreciated the opportunity to send his ten-year-old brother, Pete, somewhere during the day that would keep him out of trouble. Jonathan knew the dangers of idle hands in the rookery — having fallen into the trap himself by joining the Cobblewallers. However, his brother would not suffer the same fate if he could help it. Jonathan watched as Pete ran up to his friends, dirty blonde hair flopping over his eyes, arms waving excitedly to greet the strange woman.

Miss Taylor. That's what the children called her.

A woman who didn't belong in his neighborhood. Devil's Haven earned its name honestly by the crooks, thieves, and crime lords who ran it, and Jonathan ought to know seeing as he was in the thick of it nightly.

He'd categorize Miss Taylor as another do-gooder trying to use charity to further her own status, but he doubted anyone would view spending time in the rookery favorably. Most of the charity women turned up their noses at the smell and muck, preferring to keep their good works within the safe boundary of Peel Park where they lived.

Catching sight of him, Pete ran over. "I'm surprised to see you here; is something wrong?"

"No, I thought I'd see who this Miss Taylor is that you've been raving about." Pete had told him of a woman who'd started coming to read to the children in replacement of Father Beck's daughter, but he'd assumed it was some old biddy — not a beautiful, young woman. Truthfully, he'd been present for every reading since he first saw her last Tuesday, and after his run-in with Jasper earlier, he could use her particular brand of sunshine even if it was from afar.

"She's a fine lady. Much nicer than ole Miss Crenshaw," Pete said, his nose wrinkling in distaste. Jonathan held back a grin at the mention of the new schoolteacher. Pinched cheeks and a sharp tone to match her strict rules, she wasn't a favorite of her students. He could see why the children would flock to Miss Taylor — a vibrant ray of light in comparison.

"That's good to hear, but remember Miss Crenshaw is teaching you important skills that will help you leave Devil's Haven."

"Why would I want to leave? It's not so bad."

"It's a big world, Pete, don't you want to explore it? Have some of those adventures Miss Taylor describes?" They were on chapter four of *Alice's Adventures in Wonderland* which was filled with nonsensical happenings, but if he could use it to encourage Pete to see beyond the rookery, he would.

The last thing he wanted to happen was Pete following his footsteps and being drafted into the Cobblewallers which meant he needed the formal education Jonathan lacked. *And I need a stable income outside my pay from Lucien.*

"Mr. Travers, will you be joining us?" Pete and he responded to the feminine call of Miss Taylor as she sat on the crumbling edge of the fountain, the book open on her lap and an expectant look on her face. Her blue gaze met his eyes briefly before dropping down to Pete and motioning him over. Once everyone settled, she began, making the children laugh by using different voices for the outlandish characters.

He sank into the shadows of the alley to avoid further detection. Leaning against the worn brick, he crossed his arms over his chest and stood mesmerized by her animated storytelling. It was clear this was more than just a good deed to her; she relished the reading as much as the children enjoyed listening.

Too soon, a half-hour passed like grains of sand in a timer, trickling down faster and faster as it neared the end. When Miss Taylor finished the chapter, she shut the book with a snap and leaned forward, asking the children what they thought would happen next. An answer was never ridiculed; she listened as if the words held weight despite coming from a ragamuffin born in the slums. And when it was time for her to leave, a harsh scolding never left her lips as grubby arms hugged her legs in farewell.

Unlike any other lady who dared frequent Devil's Haven.

He watched her speak with Pete for a moment before waving good-bye, and again, he was struck by her peculiarity. Jonathan couldn't wrap his mind around the woman, but he knew of something else he wouldn't mind wrapping around her. *That'll never happen.* A genteel lady, no matter how progressive, wouldn't deign to let a street urchin like him touch her.

If he weren't so determined to turn over a new leaf due to Pete, things might be different. Proper manners wouldn't matter. Social classes would be relegated to the dung heap, and Jonathan would take what he wanted — consequences be damned.

But that's your selfishness talking. You're trying to be better now.

Watching the delectable sway of Miss Taylor's backside as she left, he allowed himself one last fantasy of having her beneath him before casting it aside until her next visit and heading home himself. Straightening, he exited the alley, nodded farewell to Pete, and walked the cobbled street until he arrived at his humble abode. The building had laid in ruins, marked for demolition years ago, yet he'd managed to purchase the deed for a song when the city didn't want to bother with the cost of tearing it down.

He had dreams of making it habitable again and offering it as a safe, affordable boarding house. Originally, the plan had come from a desire to grow a small empire like Lucien, full of diverse business exploits to see him flush with cash. Now, it served a different purpose — the key to providing a decent living for his family without Lucien's interference. After two years of ownership, the time of endless repairs neared its end, but he didn't feel relief. His boss wouldn't let him go easily, and the day of that reckoning was quickly approaching. However, several rooms needed finishing before he could start finding tenants anyway, so he'd bide his time.

Stepping inside the finished foyer, he hung his jacket on a hook by the door before taking the stairs to the second level. Heading to his private washroom, Jonathan turned the handles to begin filling a large copper tub before pulling off his dirty clothing and tossing them to the floor. This was a luxury he couldn't resist purchasing once he and Pete had moved to the second floor.

They used to live on the lower level, but after almost being killed in his sleep by falling debris a few years ago, he'd made it a priority to renovate the second-story as quickly as possible. Now the floor stood sturdy while the ceiling above lay covered, and the second and third floors could actually be accessed.

It had taken time and a considerable amount of money to get piped water in this part of town, but clean water was essential to healthy living, and it had become a necessity after a bout of cholera swept through the rookery.

Tub near to overflowing, Jonathan sank into the hot water, a tired sigh escaping as the night caught up to him. Soon, he'd be clean and could sleep before having to start the cycle all over again, but he wouldn't think about that now.

Instead, he took the bar of soap and scrubbed his body and head, making sure to rinse off the grime of the night and morning. Once finished, he closed his eyes for a moment and let his head fall back against the edge of the tub, lazily running his hand down his chest to stroke his cock. *One good spend, then off to bed.*

A vision of blonde waves floated in his mind's eye, tickling his skin and heightening his awareness of the female body he imagined draped over him. A hum of approval vibrated through him as he tightened his grip and followed the dream of Miss Taylor into oblivion.

CHAPTER TWO

The savory aroma of dinner rose from the table laden with food as Hazel swept into the dining room several minutes past seven. She'd lost track of time writing again, and judging by the frown on Mrs. Kilney's face, it'd been noticed.

"It's about time. Where have you been?" Mr. Kilney asked from his seat at the head of the table. Grey tufts of hair sat on his balding head, catching the light from the chandelier above. A gold timepiece rested in his hand before he let it drop back to his lapel and eyed her pointedly.

"I apologize for my tardiness. I was in the middle of a particularly engrossing scene of my book when I realized my error," Hazel said. Skirting around the table, she settled across from Mrs. Kilney, trying to appear contrite with folded hands in her lap and face downcast.

"See that it doesn't happen again. As a guest, we'd hoped for more respect," Mrs. Kilney said. Hazel nodded in chagrin, her cheeks heating in embarrassment. They were right to expect better behavior considering their generosity. But she'd always been easily enthralled, constantly losing awareness of time and place once in the throes of her imagination.

"Yes, ma'am," Hazel agreed, and the difficult moment passed as their plates were filled by one of the maids. Quiet sounds of chewing and silverware clinking filled the room before Mr. Kilney cleared his throat.

Dabbing a cloth serviette on his mouth, he eyed Hazel with concern. Apprehension tightened in her chest at the severity of his expression. "It's come to my attention that you've been spending your afternoons volunteering in Devil's Haven. I'm not sure it's a good idea for you to be traipsing through that part of town alone...or at all. It's not safe or proper; I doubt your father..."

"My father would've approved. He was an educator first and believed everyone deserved the opportunity to learn." A scholar by trade, her father's specialty had been horticulture and botany, thus the names of his four daughters: Hazel, Lily, Iris, and Caraway. Unlike most fathers, he encouraged them to pursue their academic interests and didn't discriminate because they were girls.

"That may be true but in an educational setting — not in one of the most unsavory parts of Manchester. A young, unescorted woman like yourself will be a magnet for trouble. Anything could happen to you." The familiar warning rankled. First her sisters, and now the Kilneys. Did no one trust her to take care of herself?

Hazel knew better than anyone how to handle her life. The accident may have prompted unexpected attacks when she became overwhelmed with guilt or fear, but she managed those episodes with aplomb. Pursuing her creative ambition, gaining steady employment, and volunteering — all those activities kept them at bay.

"Father Beck deemed it safe enough for his daughter before I took over. Surely the approval of a curate outweighs any concerns." She tried a different tact — appealing to their Christian duty.

"Yes," Mrs. Kilney continued. "But questionable men still abound..."

While her face remained neutral during the lecture, her mind glazed over and wandered back to the rookery, remembering the pair of green eyes spying on her when she'd called for Peter to join the group.

Speaking of questionable men.

She'd never seen the stranger in the alley before, but his gaze stayed tethered to her the entire time as if they were somehow connected. *Fanciful thinking.* Something she'd been accused of often enough.

As a child, fantastical stories with mythical creatures came naturally to her, and while the Taylor family accepted her outlandish ideas, Hazel knew that they could also be exasperating when she became too caught up in her imagination instead of doing chores, for example.

But the man's scrutinizing gaze intrigued her. She supposed it should scare her to capture a man's attention in Devil's Haven; it would certainly cause the Kilneys to lock her up in a fit of horror. Yet, fear hadn't been the emotion bubbling inside her. There'd been an answering curiosity, to know his story and why he stood separate from the group listening to her reading. And after learning from Peter it was the elusive brother he bragged about constantly, the older sibling he adored, anything resembling fear seemed out of place.

"Excuse me, Miss Taylor. Are you listening?" Mr. Kilney asked, breaking Hazel out of her musings. *Right, time to focus on the conversation at hand.*

"Of course! I appreciate both of your concerns, but I practice caution every time I enter Devil's Haven. You have nothing to worry about." She smiled brightly, hoping to allay any more discussion of the topic. It wore on her that people considered her so fragile and naive to the dangers of the world.

At three and twenty, she'd survived a dreadful accident, uprooted her life in Hampshire to start over in a new city, and procured employment. What more did she have to do to prove she was a strong, capable woman no matter how fantastical her imagination may be?

THE STENCH OF UNWASHED people and sewage ran rampant as Hazel hurried to another reading session days later — the smell commonplace in one of the most downtrodden and dangerous neighborhoods in Manchester. Taking shallow breaths to avoid the noxious fumes, she worked her way past homeless beggars, heart breaking for their plight. She'd learned on her first journey through this street not to make eye contact and walk as purposefully as possible or else risk being accosted by calls for spare change. At first, giving had been easy until it became obvious she'd never have enough funds to aid everyone, especially not on her wages from the library.

"Miss Taylor!" Hazel's eyes found Jimmy Hounds waving his arms to grab her attention. His threadbare clothing hung off a thin frame, covered in so much dirt and grime that the original color was difficult to determine. Unfortunately, Jimmy was one of the healthier looking children. Although the factories employed thousands of people, the pay wasn't always enough to maintain all the families, especially when four or five children were involved. Hazel tried her best to provide some education and entertainment in lieu of actual financial help.

"Jimmy, I'm so glad to see you. Are the rest of the children gathered?" Movement to the left of them caught her eye, and she saw the same man from before.

Jonathan Travers.

According to Peter, Mr. Travers worked odd hours, yet he chose to attend another reading. The man clearly cared for his brother by Peter's clean appearance and obvious affection, so perhaps this was just another way for him to see to his brother's welfare?

"Yes, miss. All sitting nice-like, waiting for you." Jimmy's voice distracted her as they arrived at their destination. Smiling at the gathered group, she tried to concentrate. Speculation about Mr. Travers filled her head as she found her gaze drawn towards the alley opening hoping to catch another glimpse of him.

"Hello, children. Are you all ready to continue *Alice's Adventures in Wonderland*?" Unable to make out more than a shadow, she sighed and took her place on the edge of the fountain. "The Caterpillar and Alice..." Soon enough, the story twined around her and the children, pushing away anymore thoughts of the mysterious Mr. Travers.

It's for the best...

She didn't have time to daydream about a mysterious stranger.

After an hour of reading, it was time for the children to return to their homes or school, if they were lucky enough to afford it, and the afternoon library shift awaited her. Adjusting the strap of her satchel, Hazel's neck and shoulders tensed in dread, not looking forward to the disapproving frown she was sure to receive from Mr. Kilney. Though, the comforting atmosphere of leather and ink would smooth over her agitation along with dreaming up new scenes for her book. Images of sparkling fairies flying over a field of daisies cropped up, and she immersed herself in the vision. The tension drained away as she followed her usual route home.

An alley appeared to Hazel's right, and as she passed, a dirty hand reached out to yank her inside. A scream stuck in her throat at the sudden move while another hand covered her mouth.

"Gotcha!" A male voice sounded by her ear while a second man followed them into the shaded passageway. She kicked at her attacker, heavy skirts flying up, but the man hoisted her closer and warned, "I wouldn't do that if I were you. Tommy's got a knife, and a cut by him won't stop us from having our fun with you."

"A fine bit of fluff, right, Les?" Tommy asked, smacking his lips. Disgust mixed with fright, but those emotions seemed at a distance as a sense of surreality settled over her. *Is this really happening?*

She'd already survived one near-death experience. Is it possible she found herself in another? Laughter burst from her at the absurd notion.

"What's wrong with her?"

The man loosened his arms in confusion, and she tried taking advantage of the moment by flailing her arms to land a hit. Unfortunately, they moved as if being dragged through molasses, heavy and slow, nothing for her attacker to fear.

What would the heroine in all of her writings do? *Shout, call for help, do something!* But nothing came out. She was stuck under that broken carriage again, pinned beneath pieces of wood and desperate to inhale a full breath of air — suffocating.

I can't breathe.

Suddenly, the men shoving her against the brick wall weren't her main concern as she gasped for air. *This wouldn't happen in my story* — the hysterical notion blazed clearly before blinking out. Strangled sounds erupted as she clawed at her neck, covered by sturdy cotton.

"Stop that!" Les shook her while a look of horror passed over his grimy face.

"Why's she doing that?"

"Hell if I know. She looks possessed, tetched in the head." Les threw her down to the ground as both men backed away, making the sign of the cross on their chests. "Let's get out of here."

Their pounding footsteps faded to nothing as Hazel lay in a heap on the chilled cobblestones. Something wet coated one cheek, a mix of tears and a leftover puddle from the earlier rain perhaps. Forcing stiff fingers to her throat, she struggled to unbutton the tiny clasps that bound her tighter than a fish in a sailor's net until the fabric separated, and she could take a deep breath, choking on the rush of oxygen.

Coughing and trembling, she closed her eyes, uncaring about safety and the wisdom of staying where she'd almost been violated. *Just a moment...* She'd be fine in a minute — recovered and able to make her way home.

"I found her!" Someone shouted before a shadow fell over the alley, blocking the remaining dull light. A rough hand brushed her cheek and sent a shiver down her spine.

"Don't worry, sunshine. You're safe now." A pinprick of recognition seeped into the bubble of numbness that surrounded her. That low, gravel-toned voice belonged to Peter's older brother. Lashes parting, she saw the concern in Mr. Travers's green gaze along with something dark and foreboding. "Pete, send the children home. I'll see to Miss Taylor."

"But..."

"Go, Pete. We'll meet at home when you're done," he said with more force before gentling his words when his focus returned to Hazel. "You'll be all right, Miss Taylor. Let's get you out of this alley, then I'll see you home safe and sound."

His arms worked their way under her prone body, cradling her to a firm chest, before rising and striding out to the main thoroughfare. Clenching a handful of his jacket, she tucked her face into his neck to avoid the examining stares of the children congregating on the street. The fresh scent of mint brought clarity, pushing the numbing fog from her mind and returning her to the present. Inhaling deeply, a heady jolt of relief made her blood tingle.

I'm safe. I can breathe.

Logically, it may not be smart to relax her defenses so quickly, but all she could hear in her head was the excited praise from Peter when it came to his brother. All she could see was how clean and healthy Peter looked compared to the other children, and she had to believe that was due to the care of Mr.

Travers. Surely, a man kind with children wasn't someone to fear.

It didn't take long before they stepped through the doorway of his home, and he placed her on a wooden chair pushed against the wall.

Scarcity defined the room. Walls devoid of frames, bare floors with no rugs to warm them, and this lone chair that seemed like an afterthought. Surely a small table or portrait of the family wouldn't be remiss.

Kneeling on one knee before her, he rubbed a hand over her arm before asking, "I know as far as introductions go, this isn't ideal, but I'm Pete's brother, Jonathan Travers. How are you feeling? Can you tell me what happened?"

Swallowing hard to erase the dryness in her throat, she relayed the past half-hour's events as succinctly as she could, afraid to dwell too long on the ordeal lest her body decided to revert to its panicked state.

"Do you recall what they looked like?"

"Their names were Tommy and Les, about average height." She shrugged at the lack of description as a flash of annoyance shot through her. A potential author should always pay attention to details. "I suppose that could describe a dozen men."

"No, you've done well. The rookery's a small place, and there are ways to make people talk. I'll find them."

"But for what purpose? I wasn't truly harmed. They let me be after..." She trailed off, unwilling to share her weak response to the attack.

"They shouldn't have touched you. That's reason enough to track them down," he growled, his strong response sparking a strange tingle of awareness in her belly. "I hope you see now how unsafe it is for you here. You were fortunate this time."

His eyes studied her face before dropping lower, something catching his attention. Glancing down, she noticed her dress gaping open from earlier and exposing the tops of her chemise-covered breasts. A flush of red bloomed while a gasp rose from her. Raising a hand to hastily refasten the buttons, she met his larger one lingering over the bottom button.

"Allow me."

She knew she shouldn't. It was vastly inappropriate. But after saving Hazel from a much worse fate to her virtue, mustering a care for propriety proved difficult. Besides, his steady hands methodically working their way up her body, shielding the vulnerable skin, soothed something inside she couldn't name.

Like he was fully capable of putting her back together again after she'd torn herself apart. Which was absurd; she hardly knew the man. Yet, there it was — a feeling of protection and relief from letting him care for her in such a minor way.

With the top button returned to its rightful place, Mr. Travers stood and walked to the opposite wall, the furthest he could get from her in the room. He cleared his throat and ran a hand through waves of blonde hair in need of a cut.

I could do it. The fanciful idea drifted into her addled brain, remembering watching her mother cut her father's hair.

"If you're feeling better, I'll walk you home."

She nodded and smoothed a hand over her skirt before standing, bracing a hand on the back of the chair for balance when a delayed aftereffect of her episode caused her to sway.

Mr. Travers rushed forward, arms out to catch her, but she shook her head in denial.

"I'm fine. Just stood too quickly, but I'll be able to walk home." Eyes closing briefly, she forced calming thoughts to the forefront. Mr. Kilney would be expecting her, especially now that she was late for her shift. She couldn't afford to tarry any longer, no matter how oddly comforting she found Mr. Travers's presence.

"Perhaps I should call for a hackney —"

"No, please. There's no need for such a conveyance. It'll do me good to clear my head with a brisk bit of exercise." The short interlude finally began to fade to a dull dream the more time passed, and she exhaled a sigh of relief.

A skeptical look entered his gaze, but he gestured for her to precede him out the door without a word. They walked in companionable silence, both lost in their own thoughts, until a nagging question prompted her to ask, "How did you know I needed rescue?"

"Your path leads by one of the children's homes. She saw what happened and ran back yelling for help. I happened to overhear."

"How fortunate...I appreciate your willingness to step in," she said, wondering how long she would've laid on the ground before recovering without assistance. "Some people would've ignored a little girl, not wanting to involve themselves in trouble."

He chuckled and shot a rueful smile towards her. "You don't know me very well, but I'm no stranger to trouble. Besides, I couldn't let Pete's favorite teacher be harmed."

"That's a peculiar description." She tilted her head in contemplation. They were nearing the respectable part of town and would soon arrive at their destination. Curious stares followed their progression, but Hazel ignored them. "I only read to them a couple times a week. I wouldn't call that teaching."

"I've attended a couple of these gatherings, and you do more than that. You ask them their thoughts, get them to look deeper into meanings. Sounds like teaching to me."

"You're quite the observant man, Mr. Travers."

It sounded like he muttered something akin to "You have no idea" under his breath, but she wasn't quite sure, and before she could question him, they stopped at the bottom of the steps leading to the library entrance. Turning to face each other, they waited as if expecting the other to speak first.

"You live at the library?"

"We made it."

Embarrassed laughter followed as they looked anywhere but the other. Trying again, Hazel said, "In a way. I live next door with the Kilneys who own the library. Thank you for escorting me all this way and for your aid earlier. If there's anything I can do in return..."

He shook his head and stepped back. "No need for any of that; just be more careful. Perhaps by staying out of Devil's Haven, hmm?"

Despite his warning, she would return to the rookery, increasing the odds of their paths crossing again. After all, what was the point in wallowing in fear? She'd survived as she'd done once already. Best to focus on practical matters like an acceptable explanation for her tardiness since she didn't want Mr. Kilney to forbid her from returning to Devil's Haven.

The tinkling bell over the library door went off signaling a patron exiting. Hazel looked up to see a woman and her two children departing, and when she looked back to Mr. Travers, he was gone. Her brows crinkled in disappointment at the lack of a farewell, but perhaps it was better this way.

It wouldn't do for her to be seen with a strange man outside her home and place of employment. The Kilneys adhered to a strict set of society's rules and etiquette. Unmarried women escorted by unknown men? Not the type of association they'd want of their employee and guest.

She took a deep, fortifying breath before ascending the steps. *Time to set Mr. Travers aside. He's not for you.*

CHAPTER THREE

S leet soaked through Jonathan's overcoat and dripped off the brim of his hat, but the fury in his blood kept him warm as he waited across the street from the Old Boar's Tavern, keeping an eye on the patrons retiring for the night. It hadn't taken long for him to discover the identities of the men who attacked Miss Taylor yesterday. Tom Hinckley and Les Miller were low-rung troublemakers that even Lucien wouldn't associate with, and he had bottom-of-the-barrel standards when it came to his henchmen.

A self-deprecating chuckle left Jonathan. *I should know.*

Finally, the tavern door opened, and the two bastards stumbled out, drunk on their feet. *No matter.* They'd remember his warning come morning. Abandoning his post, Jonathan followed the pair for a few minutes, putting distance between them and any lingering witnesses from the ale house.

You shouldn't be here. It's none of your business.

Yet, Miss Taylor's pale face of terror haunted his dreams along with a sense of possession he had no right to feeling, urging him to avenge her attack. A trail of mistakes shadowed his footsteps, a mountain of choices he couldn't take back or fix. Like the events leading up to his parents' deaths and their effects on Pete.

But this? Exacting revenge on Miss Taylor's behalf? Something he understood and could do well. Once satisfied with their privacy, Jonathan ran up behind the men, intent on his violent task — the old Jonathan rearing its beastly head. Shoving Tommy into the brick wall of a pawn shop, he saw the man stumble to the ground before turning to grab Les by the collar.

"What —"

Jonathan didn't let him finish his question. Throwing a quick punch and sweeping a leg under the man, a loud cracking sound filled the air as Les clutched his broken nose and curled into a fetal position on the ground. Tommy tried staggering to his feet, but Jonathan kicked him in the stomach which brought him back to his knees.

With the two men groaning on the sidewalk, he stood over them and growled, "This is your one warning. If I hear of you harming another woman like you did Miss Taylor, there won't be another reprieve. You'll be dead at the bottom of River Irwell."

"And who are you?" Les asked, pushing to his hands and knees.

Tommy answered first. "Don't you recognize him? He's one of the demons of Devil's Haven: Jonathan Travers, Lucien's man."

"And you'd best remember that," he said before leaving them bleeding and moaning, his duty completed.

Rubbing the knuckles of his hand, he ambled down the sidewalk, enjoying the empty streets at this hour. It hadn't taken much to convince Max to conduct business alone tonight, so he could handle Les and Tommy, but now the whole night lay ahead of him. If he were smart, he'd head home for several extra hours of sleep.

Instead, the tight walkways of Devil's Haven opened onto the wide streets of better neighborhoods as he neared the Kilney Library. *What do you think you're doing?*

Blood raced through his veins with no release and no intention of heeding common sense since it led him to Miss Taylor's home like a rabbit drawn to a snare. *Where's the harm in sneaking a peek into her world?* He doubted she'd return to Devil's Haven. She didn't belong in the rookery, even if he'd regret not seeing her again. This would count as a sort of farewell — putting to bed his incessant thoughts of her.

Looking up and down the street to find it deserted, Jonathan opened the small iron gate on the side of the building and walked around to the servants' entrance. It didn't take much to pick the lock and let himself inside, and the ease with which he was able to break in didn't sit well.

None of your concern.

Softening his footsteps, he passed several rooms before stopping at the end of the hallway, the main library revealed. Books lined the walls while shadows fell across pieces of furniture. For a moment, he forgot about Miss Taylor, in awe of the sheer magnitude of tomes. He'd never seen so many books in one place.

Tracing a hand over the exposed spines, he leaned close to study each title when an idea occurred to him. In past years he'd spent a considerable amount of time collecting manuals and consulting with laymen about his renovations, but he'd never had access to such a wealth of knowledge as this before.

Libraries were scarce in Devil's Haven, and he'd never thought to visit one. But now he knew his mistake.

The library appeared to be organized by subject, and soon enough he found a section covering architecture. Shifting to let more moonlight shine on the titles, Jonathan searched the shelves until he found *Nicholson's Practical Carpentry*. While the majority of his renovations were already finished, it couldn't hurt to double-check his work against a new resource. He pulled the book off the shelf and tucked it under his arm, a brief twinge of guilt pricking his conscience.

He didn't want Miss Taylor to get in trouble for a missing item then scoffed at the ridiculousness of that thought. The library housed hundreds of books. Who would notice one missing, let alone blame her? Besides, he'd return it when finished. Satisfied with that rationalization, he heard a clock chime twice and knew it was time to leave. He'd pressed his luck enough tonight.

Sparing a glance upward, wondering which room belonged to Miss Taylor, he resisted the urge to find out and left the way he came.

Another time...

The wayward thought crept in unbidden, but he didn't dispute it. The borrowed book would have to be returned eventually, and who knew what he might do on that occasion?

THE WAS SOMETHING about a freshly-bound book filled with pages of black and white. It reminded Hazel of when her father would receive a new parcel of tomes for his studies, and the memory filled her with a moment of happiness before sadness inevitably overshadowed it. Setting the recent release on the counter, she marked it down in the inventory ledger and continued counting the new shipment of books they'd received.

"I've heard good things about that one. Verne knows how to spin a fascinating tale." A young woman stepped forward and reached for one of the other new arrivals.

"I love Verne's earlier work, so it won't surprise me if this one becomes just as popular. How are you, Miss Beck?" Hazel had met the woman her first day at the library, and after discussing the merits of Elizabeth Gaskell's novel *North and South,* they'd become fast friends.

"Oh, you must call me Dot. Surely, we're past formalities."

Hazel smiled, agreeing with her assertion. "I believe you're right. So, what brings you by today? Don't tell me you already finished the stack of books you checked out last week."

"Oh, no, not quite." Dot waved her hand in denial. "I thought we could chat over tea while you tell me how you're faring in Devil's Haven? I've heard some good things, but I'm eager to hear your perspective."

Father Beck, a clergyman and Dot's father, regularly spent time in the rookery as did his daughter. Once Dot mentioned needing a replacement for a sort of book club she ran to occupy the children during their afternoon school break, Hazel had immediately volunteered for the job.

"Of course! Let me notify Mr. Kilney I'll be stepping out for a bit."

A quarter of an hour later, the women sat in a sitting room away from the main salon where Mrs. Kilney entertained friends. One of the maids finished setting the table for their small repast and discreetly left the room allowing them some privacy.

She hadn't had many friends growing up, most of her time spent with her sisters and Owen, the neighboring son of an earl. The lack of companionship hadn't overly concerned her, but now alone in Manchester with only the aging Kilneys as company, it was nice to have someone her own age to visit with. And a lover of books, no less!

Which reminded Hazel of another subject she wanted to broach: asking Dot's advice on her manuscript. No one else had looked at it so far, and it couldn't hurt to hear an unbiased opinion. Tabling that conversation for later, she bolstered herself for the coming discussion knowing Dot wouldn't be happy with recent events.

"So, tell me everything," Dot said as she poured steaming tea into her cup before adding a teaspoon of sugar and a dash of cream. Hazel followed suit, gathering her thoughts.

Where to begin?

"I suppose I should mention what happened yesterday..." While relaying the details of her attack and subsequent rescue, she watched as Dot's eyes widened in ever-increasing shock.

"Oh, my dear, that must have been truly terrifying." Dot stretched out a comforting hand to squeeze Hazel's arm. "How fortunate that you weren't seriously injured! I never would have forgiven myself if something happened to you. The rookery isn't always safe, but I suppose I forget that at times since I've gone there so much with Father without incident."

A golden curl escaped Hazel's chignon as she shook her head, refusing to lay any blame on her friend. "It's not your fault; please don't think so. It was a crime of opportunity and to be expected. My sisters and the Kilneys have warned enough times for me to have been better prepared, instead I let my mind wander to daydreams."

"Perhaps they're right, though. I'm all for an independent woman," Dot said, straightening her shoulders. "But walking around that part of town unchaperoned may test the limits of *safe* independence — no matter your vigilance or lack thereof."

Hazel scoffed. "Nonsense. I'll admit it wasn't my finest hour, but nothing truly irrevocable happened. I'm sitting here now, perfectly safe and whole. No, next time, I'll direct my attention to my surroundings and not the clouds."

"Next time? You plan on going back?"

"Naturally! The children still require attention, and I'm not one to cower." Hazel kept a neutral expression as she sipped her Earl Grey tea, the embodiment of nonchalance.

"You're braver than I," Dot said. "But I will let Father know of the altercation. Perhaps he can have the men apprehended or have someone keep watch over you."

"Thank you, but that won't be necessary." She waved a dismissive hand at the suggestion. Perhaps the carriage accident had permanently damaged her response to mortal danger, but rehashing the attack wouldn't serve any purpose. She'd take the threat of danger more seriously and remember to bring protection — a weapon to use if ever needed.

"Can we please move on to more interesting topics? Like what should I read to the children after *Alice*?"

For a moment, silence hung heavy, and Dot looked ready to argue, but in the end, she only sighed and launched into the benefits of several books. Hazel relaxed in her seat, pleased with the reprieve, and focused on this new turn in the conversation.

Devil's Haven and its threats could wait.

CHAPTER FOUR

"**Y**ou're back." Disbelief laced Jonathan's tone at seeing Miss Taylor again — her golden presence illuminating the otherwise grey landscape of the square. Nearly a week had passed since her last visit, but right on time, she showed up for her routine reading as if nothing was amiss.

Yet, everything was *amiss*. Most clearly her sense of preservation.

When Pete had run to notify him of Miss Taylor's return, he'd been flabbergasted and tailed the boy outside to see for himself. Sure enough, she stood in front of the fountain with a few of the children, reassuring them of her well-being.

Stalking closer when she didn't reply, he asked another question, irritation written on his face. "Did you learn nothing?"

"Of course not! I learned never to forget my father's pistol again." She lifted her reticule where he assumed said pistol was being held. Some of the children gasped and clambered to see it up close, prompting Miss Taylor to realize the inappropriateness of such a topic for young ears. She moved closer towards him and waved the children off for some privacy.

"You're carrying a weapon? Show me." He couldn't believe the foolhardiness of this woman. Instead of avoiding the scene of her attack, she decides the best reaction is to come back with a bloody weapon! It boggled his mind and solidified the notion that she was unlike any woman he'd ever met.

Glancing surreptitiously around as if someone would snatch the pistol the moment it's revealed, Miss Taylor pulled it halfway out before dropping it back in the bag.

"Christ! That's not going to do much for you. How old is that rusted piece of metal?"

Jerking back, her nose wrinkled, affronted at the insult. "Age has no bearing. It worked well enough when I practiced."

An agitated hand ran through his hair at the image of her practicing, the thought of her shooting tin cans or some other poor object almost laughable, if he weren't so concerned with it backfiring on her. "You're more liable to harm yourself than a criminal. Where did you say you were from again?"

"I didn't, but since you asked so nicely..." She teased, a smile tilting the corners of her pretty mouth, and the beautiful sight almost made him forget his objective. *Almost.* "The answer is Shoreham, Hampshire — a quaint country village in the south."

His eyes travelled over her hearty curves, and the answer cleared up a handful of questions he'd had. The picture of a country maiden with blonde curls and blue eyes — it was no wonder she lacked the sense to avoid Devil's Haven despite her trouble. He figured the most dangerous thing she ever encountered in Hampshire was probably a loose cow or something of that nature.

Gesturing towards the restashed pistol, Jonathan said, "Well, that's not going to do much for you here."

"It shall serve as a deterrent in the future. Surely, any criminal with an ounce of common sense would turn tail and run in the face of a barrel pointed towards them."

"You give too much credit." Arms crossing over his chest to resist shaking sense into the woman, Jonathan's chin dipped in rebuttal. "Most men will see you with your ladies' derringer and laugh, taking it as a challenge to disarm the woman who thought she could best him." A few of those types popped into his head even as he warned her.

"And that would be their mistake." A mulish expression wiped away her previously lighter attitude, yet somehow, he found it just as adorable. *Stupid sod.*

An argument sat on the tip of his tongue when Pete joined them. "We're all here, Miss Taylor. Will we be starting soon?"

Turning around, she nodded. "Yes, I think your brother and I have finished here." She raised a brow as if to dare him to refute her claim, but Jonathan remained quiet, turning his thoughts to alternative avenues for protection if she insisted on defying him.

He dropped into a mocking bow, brandishing an arm to the side. "Indeed. We'll continue this conversation at a later time." Pete looked between them confused by the obvious tension but shrugged his shoulders before dragging Miss Taylor to the waiting group.

Jonathan leaned against the icy bricks of the building behind him working through possible solutions. First, he'd hire someone to start following her in secret. This would serve the dual purpose of protection while also providing updates on her whereabouts outside Devil's Haven — something he was intensely curious about no matter how foolish it made him.

Gaze shifting from Miss Taylor to the huddled forms sitting on the cobblestones, their breaths rising in the chilly air, another problem became obvious. Winter would befall Manchester soon, and he worried about them being exposed to such elements. There wasn't a doubt in his mind that if thugs couldn't stop Miss Taylor from her duties, inclement weather wouldn't either. However, she wasn't heartless; she wouldn't want the children to suffer.

Searching for answers, he let his mind wander, though his stare never did. Slender fingers turned thin pages and cheeks pinkened from excitement and the brisk breeze. Everything about Miss Taylor drew him like a moth to flame, yet he couldn't pinpoint why. It went beyond physical charms; he'd seen plenty of beautiful women in his day and never had he felt this pull.

"Mr. Travers, enjoying the reading, as well, are you?" Dr. Robert Forrester joined him, following his gaze. "I heard through the grapevine that Miss Taylor had a mishap on her last visit. Good to see she wasn't harmed."

A tenuous friendship had formed between the two men after the doctor had patched Jonathan up after the falling debris incident. Usually, the man's wife, Mrs. Johanna Forrester, worked alongside him and caused most of the friction as Jonathan couldn't resist flirting with her to ruffle the doctor's feathers. It was all in good fun, though. He knew the two were a devoted pair, and his true interest lay elsewhere. Specifically, a couple yards away in a grey cotton dress that molded to her voluptuous body.

"Not yet, anyway," Jonathan grumbled, eliciting a chuckle from Forrester.

"I see. Not used to handling a stubborn woman, Travers? My Johanna will be delighted to hear about this new development."

Jonathan sneered at the assumption. "There's no *new development*. Just a woman who doesn't know what's right for her own good."

"But you'd be happy to tell her?" Forrester guessed, rubbing a hand over his mouth but failing to cover the amused smirk. Clearly, his dilemma provided the afternoon's entertainment for the usually taciturn man.

"Don't you have some poor, ailing soul to see?" Jonathan ignored the gibe, unwilling to add more fuel to the fire. Let the man find diversion elsewhere.

Forrester hummed in agreement and clasped Jonathan's shoulder in commiseration before parting with a "Good luck to you."

Luck's not what I need.

No, he needed to understand what drove Miss Taylor. Why risk herself for a couple of hours a week with rookery children? It didn't make sense. And he knew he wouldn't be satisfied until he figured it out.

Miss Taylor embodied mystery. One he was determined to solve.

CHAPTER FIVE

"A word, Miss Taylor," Jonathan said as he stepped from the shadows two days later, awaiting her visit. A brush of heat stroked over her skin at his appearance. Though not classically handsome with his stout build and overlong blonde hair, a rough magnetism clung to him, making Hazel itch to touch.

Fight the temptation. Act like a lady. Ladies don't yearn to touch men who are not their betrothed even if he did rescue you like the hero in a penny dreadful.

"I'm afraid the children are expecting me, Mr. Travers. Perhaps afterwards." Hazel sidestepped him, studiously ignoring the delicious scent that beckoned her closer, as she continued towards the ruined fountain where a smattering of children already clustered together.

"It pertains to your insistence on visiting Devil's Haven. I have a proposition for you."

Breath stuttering in her lungs, various ideas rolled around in her imagination — each possibility of what he'd want from her becoming more elaborate and decidedly unladylike. *Control yourself.* But it was difficult when she'd never experienced urges like this before. The men in the village never evoked such a strong response.

"What did you have in mind?"

"If you'll follow me, it'll take but a moment and you'll see what I mean."

Curiosity getting the best of her, they bypassed the fountain to the confused looks of Mary and Jimmy and arrived at Mr. Travers's home. The building stood out from its ramshackle neighbors — shining with fresh repairs — and exhibited a depth of care that exceeded her expectations. He opened the door and led her to the first room on the right. A desk sat at the front of the room while a few mismatched chairs lined one wall.

"What is this?"

"This is your new reading room. It'll be a mite safer than sitting out on the streets, not to mention provide protection from the elements when the weather turns."

Hazel walked around the room, her hand drifting over painted walls, the smell of turpentine still floating around the space despite an open window for ventilation. She knew from Peter that his brother had been working for years to remodel this building, but she never expected him to offer her and the children refuge. The kind gesture warmed her, and again she wondered at what sort of man he was.

"I'm not sure how this provides protection for me as I come and go, but I appreciate the shelter from the rain and cold." Already the November temperatures dipped low enough to show her breath. It wouldn't be long before snow and ice followed, and the ragged garments worn by the children wouldn't offer much defense against such conditions.

"Your protection is a bit more symbolic. Everyone will know that if they harm you, they'll have to deal with me." He watched her inspect the room from the doorway, one broad shoulder resting against the frame. Finishing a turn about the room, she halted in front of him, bewilderment scrunching her brows.

"Why are you doing this for me?"

"It's not for you," he denied, avoiding her gaze. "It's for my brother and all the other little vagabonds who prefer to spend their school break listening to you rather than go home. It'd break their hearts to see you harmed. This space was sitting here empty, so you might as well put it to good use since you've decided to risk yourself coming back." He tugged on the sleeve of his jacket in discomfort before shoving fidgety hands into his pockets.

A small grin tugged on her mouth at his explanation. She doubted he'd ever admit to actually caring about the welfare of those *vagabonds* despite actively trying to create a safe place for their families to live. Peter's summary of what Mr. Travers hoped this building would become flashed in her mind.

What an enigma you are.

Edging closer to join him near the doorway, she said, "Well, whatever your reason, I thank you, and I'm sure the children will be grateful." Rising to her toes on impulse, she placed a hand on his shoulder before kissing his stubbled cheek. The peck intended to be innocent — a gesture of gratitude — yet she found herself lingering, enjoying the proximity to him.

"Miss Taylor..." A warning. His hot breath sent a shiver down her body, and suddenly she ached to know what a real kiss from him would feel like. All her previous excuses for denying such sinful urges flying out the window. A reckless longing flitted through her body. A need to know for herself.

If I dare...

Slowly, afraid that he'd break the moment and ruin her chance, Hazel drew her cheek along his until their mouths met, a delicate brushing of lips, before she pressed more firmly into him.

They stood there — frozen. Nothing spectacular happened, and disappointment cooled some of her ardor.

But just as she started to push away, something changed. One of Mr. Travers's hands cupped her bottom in a most indecent way as his other hand tangled in her hair causing a stinging sensation at the slight pull. His head shifted slightly, then a low whisper caressed her sensitive nerves. "Open for me, sunshine."

The rough demand rekindled her curiosity, and it occurred to her that he knew more about kissing than she did — perhaps she should listen. Assenting to his request, anticipation infused their shared breath. The intimacy of such a simple act shook her and a seed of doubt, of being out of her depth, began to take root.

What am I doing? How could I...

Mr. Travers nipped at her bottom lip, putting a halt to the spiraling thoughts. "Focus on me," he said as if she'd spoken her fears aloud. Her gaze clashed with his before the gap between them closed and his tongue swept inside to caress hers.

Flush against his firm body, heat blazed in her veins, burning a trail down to her core and tearing a moan from her throat. This bore no resemblance to her pitiful attempt at kissing. It was more than mouths meeting in unison. It was a sort of sharing — a give and take.

Mr. Travers tightened his hold, his hands clenching tightly, and she reciprocated by wrapping a gloved hand behind his neck and pulling him closer, eliciting his own sound of pleasure. Excitement bubbled over as a feminine awareness settled over her skin.

She may not be experienced. This may be her first kiss. Yet, she held as much power over him as he did her; she only lacked the skill to wield it as proficiently. *But not for long.*

Mimicking his movements, she parried when he retreated, all the while floating in an ocean of desire. She'd read romantic novels, wished for a hero, but none of that compared to being held by a flesh and blood man who wanted her: Hazel Anne Taylor, not some fictional heroine. And it thrilled her.

"Miss Taylor..." The two of them broke apart at Peter's fading voice. She swallowed hard and brought a glove to her swollen lips, sparing a glance at the boy to gauge his reaction. "I'm sorry. I didn't mean —"

"It's all right, Pete. Miss Taylor will be right out." Inquisitive eyes roamed over them before he nodded and ran back outside.

Wilting in relief, she returned her gaze to Mr. Travers, only to see the back of his form as his heavy tread sounded down the hallway. He certainly had a penchant for such disappearances as she recalled him leaving the same way when he left her at the library.

Confused by the dismissal, she almost called out to him but thought better of it. What did she expect to say anyway? *Thank you for the kiss, sir, but now it's time for me to do what I actually came here for?*

Groaning at the ridiculous nature of that statement, she turned in the opposite direction and hurried to tell the group of their new meeting place, like a mother hen guiding her ducklings to their nest.

Peter could be heard boasting about the work his brother had done to prepare the room, and she smiled at the pride in his voice. It was clear the boy loved and idolized his older brother — a fact that endeared Mr. Travers to her even more. And fortunately, Peter didn't seem the worse for wear after witnessing their embrace. *Thank goodness.*

She wouldn't have thought a man such as Mr. Travers would deign to insert himself in the affairs of his little sibling, yet it was obvious they shared a close bond. One that reminded her of her own sisterly ties, and she made a note to reply to Caraway's letter when she returned to the Kilneys. Their correspondence had been sorely lacking due to her concentration on starting over in Manchester, but that didn't mean she wanted to leave her sisters completely behind.

Settling at her newly-acquired desk, Hazel prompted the children to take their seats, though there weren't quite enough chairs for everyone as some ended up on the floor. But at least it was dry unlike the cobblestones outside.

Over halfway through the book now, the children were thoroughly absorbed in the story. They especially had a morbid affinity for the Queen of Hearts and her ruthless personality. Hazel tried to ignore any hidden meanings behind the fascination, though, and fixated on the positive interest in reading. She couldn't wait until she finished her own book and was able to share it. To see their faces light up in awe or laugh at some silly antics. It would make everything leading up to that moment worth it.

Buoyed by that notion, she forged ahead, immersing herself in a different world and letting her own concerns over writing and Mr. Travers fade to the background.

CHAPTER SIX

"**N**ight, Pete. I'll see you in the morning." Jonathan finished tucking his brother into bed and started to leave for the evening before remembering to check on an earlier issue. "Oh, I forgot to ask how Molly's doing after Dr. Forrester saw her."

The poor girl had slipped on a slick patch of cobblestones that produced a large, bleeding gash down her leg. He'd immediately sent for the doctor after witnessing the incident, worried she might need stitches. Miss Taylor didn't think the injury warranted such a reaction as a call to the doctor, but he figured it best to be safe rather than sorry.

"She cried while the doc sewed her up, so Miss Taylor let her sit on her lap during the reading. After that, she was fine." Yes, he'd be fine, too, if he had Miss Taylor comforting him.

He thought of their kiss.

Ill-advised. Startling. Delicious.

But it couldn't happen again. They weren't right for each other. The librarian cum author with the rookery rogue? Sounded like a penny dreadful gone wrong.

"Very well. I'm glad everything turned out okay. Good night."

A yawn garbled Pete's soft farewell, and tenderness filled Jonathan until he stepped outside to meet Max — body tensing as he prepared himself for another night of work. And seeing Lucien.

Sometimes, he wondered if it would've ever occurred to him to leave if it weren't for Pete. Jonathan remembered what it was like joining the Cobblewallers at thirteen, eager to get out from under his parents' thumbs and strike out on his own. Back then, he'd been a simple thieving boy working his way up the ranks to become Lucien's right-hand man. And while the position carried its fair share of risk, other job opportunities didn't interest Jonathan until the death of their parents placed Pete under his care.

The boarding house was supposed to be the first stepping stone towards growing an empire like Lucien's — something the man approved of as it was tacitly agreed that Jonathan would someday rule the Cobblewallers after Lucien's demise. All those plans collapsed like the building that took his parents. He didn't want to lead a rookery gang. How could he when the idea of Pete joining made his stomach turn?

"Something's up tonight," Max warned as they headed down the foggy street.

Shoving clenched fists in his coat, Jonathan considered the ominous words. "What do you mean?"

"Lucien's having us meet him at The Hen House to see Abbott instead of going on our normal rounds." The manager of the brothel Lucien owned, Abbott, was a slight man who Jonathan used to see more often when he visited The Hen House. Over the years, though, the establishment became seedier and seedier, and Jonathan preferred not to contract some kind of disease by frequenting such a place.

It wasn't long before the rundown building sandwiched between a tavern and pawn shop came into view along with Lucien who stood in front of the tavern, smoking a cheroot. Catching sight of them, he stamped it out on the ground and grinned. "Ah, my boys. Ready for a bit of fun?"

"What are we doing here?"

"Thought we'd take a turn down memory lane. Go back to the old days of working together." Lucien hooked a thumb towards the building. "You see, dear Abbott has been skimming the coffers, and it's time he remembered who he works for. That's where you boys come in."

Foreboding sank in his stomach as he recalled what exactly those old dealings entailed — bloody violence.

"And what prompted this need to reenact the past?" he asked, morbidly curious about the change in the evening's agenda.

"Rumors are swirling around about you leaving the Cobblewallers for good once your boarding house scheme is complete. Now, I know those can't be true when you're set to take over for me years from now. That business venture is only a stepping stone to add to the network of shops we run, isn't that right?"

Fuck. Who'd been bandying about his private life for all and sundry?

"The plan's changed since my parents died. Pete needs more stability. I can't offer him such a thing while dividing my time between the Cobblewallers and the boarding house. Surely, you understand." The bitter cold bit at his cheeks as they stood frozen in quiet battle. He'd wanted to broach the subject more delicately with Lucien rather than have *him* ambush Jonathan with the news.

"Hardly. You're a capable man. I practically raised you, so I should know." Lucien preened, and Jonathan resisted the urge to punch the satisfied look off his face. Raised him? He could laugh at the absurdity of the claim. "You can manage both businesses, and Pete will be the better for it. No, I think you're forgetting how much you enjoy this work. Collecting debts while sometimes adventurous doesn't provide the same thrill as your old responsibilities. But don't worry, by the end of the night, you'll remember the old Jonathan Travers."

Exactly what he was actively avoiding: being that man.

Following Lucien into the brothel, he and Max flanked his sides as they barged into Abbott's office at the back of the building. A mess stinking of stale perfume, calling the room an office was generous.

"Gentlemen! I wasn't expecting company, but please have a seat." Abbott gestured to two worn chairs. "What can I do for you?"

"For starters, you can stop stealing from me before I decide to have my men here drop you dead as a fish in the river," Lucien stated bluntly, eyes skewering his thieving manager. The man's face paled before he started sputtering nonsense in his defense.

"What? No! You must be mistaken! I've never —"

Lucien snapped his fingers and pointed. "Jonny."

Shuffling forward, feet dragging as if lead weights, he pinned Abbott to the desk in a practiced move. "I'd stop lying if I were you," he muttered under his breath.

Abbott began vehemently shaking his head. "Alright, I admit to borrowing —"

"Borrowing? Is that what they call it when an employee steals from the hand that feeds him?" Lucien clucked his tongue, sighing as if truly hurt by his manager's actions. "You're lucky I'm feeling generous tonight, and it's damned difficult finding good help these days." He pierced Jonathan with a beady glare — that last part was meant for him.

"So, you'll live to see another day," Lucien continued. "Albeit a painful one. Do it, Jonny."

Hesitation held his muscles in suspension, but he knew refusing would be worse than complying to the order. Inhaling a deep breath, Jonathan wrenched Abbott's arm higher, a violent crack of bones overshadowed only by the man's hoarse cries of shock and pain.

Nausea sickened his stomach at the offensive act. The sad part is he once wouldn't have even been affected — would've oddly enjoyed the sight of a job well-done, if not the actual hurt inflicted.

Unbidden, a picture of Miss Taylor rose to the forefront, at once comforting and abhorrent. He never wanted her connected to any of this even if only in his thoughts. She represented innocence, warmth, and kindness which was why she didn't belong in Devil's Haven or with him. Too bad his heart and mind seemed to forget such facts the moment he was in her presence.

"Good work, Jonny. Didn't that feel good?" Lucien patted him on the back as they left Abbott crying in his office, draped over the desk, arm at an awkward angle. "Now, no more talk of leaving, eh?"

Jonathan kept silent.

CHAPTER SEVEN

At their next meeting, the group of children filed out of the room until only one remained: Mary. The little girl played with the end of her braid and scuffled forward to where Hazel was also preparing to leave.

"What is it, Mary?"

"Is it hard to read?" The innocent question brought Hazel's head up, and she rounded the desk.

"It can be difficult at first learning to recognize letters and the sounds they make, but once you grasp the basics, it's fairly easy. Aren't they explaining such things at school?"

"Don't know." The girl kicked the toe of her shoe on the floor. "I can't go."

Hazel almost asked why when it dawned on her. Taking in Mary's worn dress held together by patches of mismatched fabric and her slippered feet where one of the soles was starting to flap away from the top stitching, it was clear that tuition to the local school lay out of her family's reach even if it was meant for children of the lower class.

"But you'd like to learn?" Hazel kneeled in front of the girl, so they were eye-level.

The girl nodded shyly, still playing with her hair. "Then, I'll teach you. Everyone should have the opportunity to learn how to read if they want to. Can you come back tomorrow at the same time we usually meet?"

A bright smile lit the girl's face as she jumped to give Hazel a hug. Wobbling a bit before bracing herself and returning the gesture, Hazel's sight became blurry at such enthusiasm for a simple task. Blinking rapidly to ward off more tears, she shooed Mary home and went in search of Mr. Travers after dabbing at the corners of her eyes. She'd need to check with him to see if it would be all right to use this room again for an unscheduled purpose.

Thankfully, Mr. Kilney had reluctantly granted her request for an extended recess due to her continual tardiness. It had helped that she'd reminded him of Dot's clergyman father and doing the Lord's work by educating the poor children of Devil's Haven. For a moment, she feared his Christian duty would fail her, but in the end, he'd allotted more time for her afternoon session.

Hearing voices coming from down the hall, Hazel followed the sound until she found Peter and Mr. Travers seated at a wooden table sharing a plate of biscuits between them. Their conversation stammered to a halt at her appearance, and she felt like one of the plants her father studied under his microscope as their attention turned to her.

"Apologies for the interruption. Mary asked if I could instruct her on how to read, and I suggested meeting here tomorrow. Would that be all right? I don't want to inconvenience you when you've already been so generous." She directed her question towards Mr. Travers, unsure of his response. If asked a week ago what she thought he might say, she would have immediately supposed his agreement.

However, that would've been before their kiss, and since then he'd kept himself scarce when usually he hovered in the background during reading time.

He clearly regretted the action if he'd taken it upon himself to avoid her. So, agreeing to let her spend more time in his home? That was as much of a toss-up as who would win in a race between her and Lily — the steady pace of her sister or the early sprint chosen by Hazel.

Taking a bite of a biscuit, Mr. Travers made her wait while he mulled it over. The exaggerated length of time it took for him to chew and swallow put her in mind that he was teasing her with suspense. But, surely, that was just her imagination.

"I thought you said you weren't a teacher." The smug tone of his voice proved that, yes, he was teasing her, and secondly, how grateful she was for it.

Pulling out a chair with a relieved sigh, she took a seat and snatched her own biscuit off the tin plate he offered, humming in pleasure as the buttery treat melted on her tongue. "Think of it more as a tutor."

"Semantics," he said, leaning back, his legs sprawling under the table. "Still means I'm right about what you are."

Lifting her gaze heavenward in supplication amusement mingled with a wash of guilt. Her father had been an excellent professor before retiring to research full-time. She'd never be capable of living up to his legacy, but she hoped to forge her own as an author and prove her life had been worth saving over her parents'. Every day guilt weighed on her, but she kept it at bay by focusing on accomplishing something worthwhile like publishing her book — a dream her parents had supported.

Fortunately, Peter saved her from forming a rebuttal. "Can I come, too?"

Mr. Travers tilted his head to the side, his brow furrowing in bewilderment. "Why? You know your letters."

Warmth filled Hazel at that fact, pushing away the creeping melancholy, and curiosity as to who taught Peter gnawed at her. The local school hadn't been open long enough to take full credit. Was it Mr. Travers or perhaps a parent? She'd learned through Peter that their parents had died years prior from a building collapse, but he would've been eight years old then — capable of learning.

Propping bony elbows on the tabletop, Peter dropped his chin into his hands. "Maybe I can help? Or listen? What book will you bring?"

The bombardment of questions cheered her, his enthusiasm catching. Clearly, the prospect of a new story excited Peter, and she wondered if some of the other children felt the same way — if they were all hungry for more.

"I would love for you to join us, but I haven't decided on the book yet. What do you suggest? We could learn about pirates or horses, whatever piques your interest," she said.

"What about your favorite book, Miss Taylor?" Mr. Travers interjected.

"A solid choice...Have you heard of *Little Women* by Louisa May Alcott? It's an older publication, and I've always had an affinity for it since it follows four sisters." When the Taylor sisters had discovered the novel, they'd spent many a night perusing the pages until they were worn thin — their American counterparts fascinating them.

"Another story about girls?" Peter asked, a petulant twist to his mouth causing Hazel and Travers to laugh at the mulish expression.

"Don't worry. It's only one of many options. When I return to the library, I'll see what I can find that might fit both your and Mary's tastes." Several ideas came to mind as she stole another biscuit.

"An affinity for sisters, hmm? Do you have many then?"

"Three, although technically, one's a cousin. Caraway, Iris, Lily, then me."

"You're the baby of the family — that explains it," Mr. Travers said with a shake of his head.

"Explains what?" She prepared for an insult based on his tone, though how he could fault her birth order escaped understanding.

"Everything." One by one, he began ticking off reasons with his fingers. "Why you think you're impervious to danger despite an *actual* encounter with it. Why you refuse to listen to me when I *warn* you of said danger." He emphasized certain words as if talking with a toddler, and it rankled. "I have no doubt that your family doted on you, swaddling you in a protective ball of cotton, while refusing to deny you anything you desired. Am I close?"

Hazel crushed the remaining bit of her biscuit to crumbs in an effort to maintain her composure. Brushing them off in a measured stroke, she forced a smile and leaned forward, eyes narrowed. "Perhaps, but my childhood ended years ago." Indeed, her innocence had swiftly gone the way of a puff of smoke after the carriage incident. *Or Lily's ordeal.* But either way, it didn't matter.

"Why do you say that?"

"My parents died in a carriage accident that I was also part of, so I understand how to survive. I am a grown woman who can make decisions for herself, and while I appreciate your repeated concern, I won't be swayed from my course. And if you want to get into personality traits based on birth order, let me expound on the ways *you*..."

He raised a hand in defense and shot a side glance towards Peter, reminding her that they weren't alone for this little tiff. "That won't be necessary. I assure you I'm well aware of my faults. And I didn't mean to bring up your parents; I didn't know it was a sore subject."

Swiping a cool hand over her heated cheek, embarrassment flooded through her body at losing control so quickly and in front of Peter. Her voice had risen terribly close to shrill while the unfamiliar feeling of anger built in her blood. Though not prone to explosive outbursts like Lily, every now and then she was known to release her temper like an agitated volcano.

"I apologize —"

"I'm sorry for —"

They both ceased, waiting for the other to continue, before breaking into rueful chuckles at the silent impasse. Peter hopped up from his chair and tilted his head, clearly confused by the exchange. "I should leave before I'm late for my afternoon class, if that's alright. I'll see you tomorrow, Miss Taylor."

Mr. Travers nodded his consent before rising himself and taking the now empty plate to the wash bowl on the counter. Following suit, Hazel pulled on her gloves and said, "I suppose that's my cue. Thank you for allowing me use of the room tomorrow. Will you be here to welcome us?"

"If not me, you'll meet Mrs. Wilson, our housekeeper. She comes in on Mondays, Wednesdays, and Fridays."

"Oh...I'll look forward to it." Another tidbit of information she hadn't known but should've guessed. Did she really think Mr. Travers cooked and cleaned the entire household on top of his regular duties?

As she left, it occurred to her that she didn't know much about the Travers family. The list compiled of deceased parents, a previously undisclosed housekeeper, and that Mr. Travers worked irregular hours. Information gleaned primarily from Peter.

The irregular job hours stuck with her as she pondered what he did for a living. Obviously, his boarding house wasn't open to tenants yet, so he wasn't earning a steady wage through that avenue. Most of the residents of Devil's Haven were employed by the many factories of Manchester, yet they ran on tight schedules, something Mr. Travers didn't seem to heed.

The scene of her attack came upon her sooner than she expected, making her realize once again she'd drifted off in her thoughts — something she'd promised not to do again. Quickening her step, she held her breath as she passed the alley.

Keep your mind on the walk, Hazel. You can ruminate on Travers once you're home safe.

A trembling hand closed tighter around the bag holding her father's old pistol, the small weight relieving some of her tension until it slowly released like a deflated balloon as she continued on unharmed. Upon entering the quiet library at the end of her journey, she found Mr. Kilney marking down returns.

"May I speak with you for a moment?" Hazel might as well deal with any objections he'd have to her spending more time in the rookery now. To be honest, even she was beginning to lament all the special treatment she requested — longer breaks for personal use — when Mr. Kilney had been kind enough to take her in.

"Yes, what is it?"

"I need more time off in the afternoons starting tomorrow," she said quickly, wringing her hands.

"Tomorrow? But you're not scheduled for another visit until Thursday." His brows drew together like one long hairy caterpillar on his forehead. *A fair point to mention.*

"Normally, that would be true. However, I'll be starting to teach the children their letters in addition to reading to them. Father Beck believes it's a wonderful idea." She added the fib onto the end and hoped God would forgive her for the small lie.

Mr. Kilney muttered, "He does. Does he?" Tapping his pencil against the wooden countertop, a frown marred his face. "I suppose if it's God's will, then I must abide by it."

Hazel refrained from showing any outward relief, just dipped her head in gratitude. "Thank you, sir. Truly, you exemplify the Christian standard for all of us." The flattery may be thick as molasses, but it couldn't hurt to boost his ego.

He straightened and adjusted his collar. "Yes, well...One must always follow the dictates set by God and his ministers. I'll allow the extended time, though you'll need to make up a portion of it in the evenings. I'm certainly not running a charity like Father Beck."

"Yes, sir." She curtsied and left to put away her belongings before joining him to help. The difficult part was over; now to choose a book for tomorrow, and everything would be set.

CHAPTER EIGHT

"I heard you roped George into tailing your woman throughout Manchester." Max downed the rest of his ale as the barmaid dropped another on the table with a wink. They'd decided to stop for the night at Old Boar's Tavern, though Jonathan questioned the wisdom of their choice the louder the raucous patrons became. He didn't feel like engaging with a pack of drunk bastards if they thought to earn bragging rights by besting Lucien's top two men.

"She's not my woman," Jonathan said with a snap. *Even if she does feature in my dreams every night.* He flashed back to their kiss, to the shock of her pliable mouth brushing against his without any push from him, and his first kiss from a true lady. Usually, his sexual exploits remained confined to the widows of Devil's Haven — experienced women who knew better than to expect more than a physical release from him.

The innocence displayed by the gentle touch had captured him as surely as a fish on a hook. And when she'd hesitated, unsure of what to do next? How could he resist educating her?

But all good things come to an end, and afterwards, he'd berated himself for giving in to his base desires. Nothing serious could ever develop between them. And while she might be tempted to dirty herself with him, she'd soon regret that decision which is why he'd stayed away, skipping her visits.

Especially after that night with Abbott and Lucien reminded him of how different their worlds were. But he was trying to be better and put that behind him.

Changing his life didn't include sullying a genteel lady. That's something the old, selfish Jonathan would've done without a second thought — taking what he wanted and damn the consequences. But how could he treat Miss Taylor in such a way? And with Pete observing every exchange?

"Yet you have her followed for constant protection and let her run a class out of your home. Sounds like she's yours to me." Max shrugged and continued tracking the barmaid as she made her rounds. The man clearly had plans for later that evening that didn't involve talking with Jonathan, but he wasn't wrong in his assertions.

Hell, Jonathan had agreed to letting her use his home more frequently now that she wanted to teach them how to read. It'd been impossible to refuse the sweet request.

You're a damn fool for agreeing.

As if he needed to spend more time around her lush curves and soft smiles.

"Let's forget about Miss Taylor. What am I going to do about Lucien?" Each day he inched closer to completing the boarding house renovations while a viable solution to give Lucien for his departure drifted further away. Past impulsive behaviors sprang forward. If he didn't care about Pete's well-being or even Miss Taylor's, he'd say to hell with it and leave the Cobblewallers without a backward glance especially after Lucien forced him on that bad business with Abbott.

However, present circumstances demanded finesse.

Max groaned and took another drink. "Now, that is a problem. It won't be easy breaking free from his stranglehold now that it's no secret what you're planning."

"I've done his bidding for years now — longer than anyone else in his employ. Why can't he just let me go? It's not like I'm enlisting with a rival gang." His voice lacked much hope, but he supposed Lucien could eventually relent.

And I'm the Duke of York.

Lucien had been grooming him to lead for over a decade. He wouldn't so easily release him.

A snort of commiseration left Max as he understood his trouble. Rubbing tired eyes, Jonathan sighed. "I'm fucked."

"Right you are...And now if you'll excuse me, I think I'm about to get the same, but in a much more enjoyable manner." Max tipped his head in farewell and walked towards the back of the room where the barmaid appeared to be waiting. Shoving his chair back, he tossed coins on the sticky table and left in the opposite direction.

If only I had a pretty country maiden waiting for me...

CHEERFUL CHATTER GREETED Jonathan as he answered the knocking on the door later the next afternoon. Miss Taylor and Mary stood with another little girl talking and giggling, and the image eased some of the tension tightening around his neck in preparation for their visit. They'd left yesterday in an amiable if awkward mood which only added to his muddled thoughts.

"Good afternoon, Mr. Travers! Mary brought her friend Lizzie today, and we were just discussing how excited we are to start." He stepped back as the trio swept in, making a beeline for the room to the right, and a whiff of lavender curled around him — Miss Taylor's familiar scent and one that was quickly becoming his favorite.

Before he could reply, Mrs. Wilson hurried down the hallway, wiping her hands on the old apron tied around her waist. Pete followed behind. "Welcome, welcome! You must be Miss Taylor. I'm Mrs. Ida Wilson, though my dear Frank passed away some years ago." She reached for Miss Taylor's offered hand, clasping it with both hands before letting go and continuing to babble. "How Peter's raved about you, and now we finally meet! And who might you be?"

Bent at the waist, Mrs. Wilson herded the children towards chairs near the front of the room, her infectious nature catching as the girls introduced themselves.

"She's quite a whirlwind, isn't she?" Miss Taylor placed a hand over her heart as if to catch her breath from the encounter, but an amused smile adorned her cheeks.

"Yes, but she treats us well — sees that we're fed and clean," he said. She'd been a neighbor and looked after Pete while their parents worked their shifts at the textile factory. Sometimes she felt more like a mother to Pete than their own, so when her husband died in the same incident that took their parents, it was only natural for her to follow Pete to Jonathan's home and provide a bit of structure to the boy's life.

"No small feat, I wager. Tending to a grown man and a growing boy." Eyeing him up and down as if appreciating what hearty meals and laundered clothing could do for a man, the examination twisted his insides, and when her gaze rose again to his, she paused. "Are you blushing, Mr. Travers? I apologize if my perusal made you uncomfortable..."

Now, her cheeks turned red, and he cursed. What hell the moment had become with him digressing to a youth shy of women and she the innocent miss discovering a man's form for the first time.

Escape. Now.

"It must be overly warm here. I don't blush." *Or at least I didn't before you came into my life.* "I'll leave you to your lessons. If you need anything, Mrs. Wilson shall be able to help you."

Sliding past her, he jogged up the stairs leading to his private room and paced the floor to release the ball of energy bouncing around his stomach. He wanted to go back downstairs and listen to Miss Taylor, but it wouldn't do him any good. *You must stay away*, he reprimanded himself. *Keep things polite and indifferent.* Though, he'd been failing dismally.

Spying the borrowed book he'd laid on the side table, he inhaled a harsh breath and decided if he couldn't hear Miss Taylor's gentle voice speaking to the children, he could at least educate himself with his own book.

Learning new things calmed him, and it would serve the dual purpose of pushing the beguiling blonde aside for at least an hour. Dry eyes bothered him as this was usually his time to rest, but how could he sleep with her mere feet away? It wasn't smart for him to be in a bed with her under his roof. Pleasuring himself to thoughts of her while she sat unaware downstairs rubbed him the wrong way.

Yes, because she'd prefer it if you waited until after she left. He allowed a brief self-deprecating smile before wiping it away.

"In the art of building..." The first words on the page echoed in his mind as he devoted himself to learning and not thinking about Miss Taylor.

The slamming of a door broke Jonathan's concentration an hour or so later marking the end, he assumed, of the lesson. Closing the book with a scrap of fabric holding the page, he stood and stretched before heading downstairs to check on Pete. *Then, sleep.*

A yawn overtook him to punctuate the point. At the bottom of the stairs, he was about to call for Pete when he stopped, stunned to see Miss Taylor hunched over the old desk he'd rummaged to find. What was she still doing here? Nearing her, he noticed sheets of paper scattered on the desk filled with scribblings and drawings.

"What's all this?"

She jerked back, dropping the pencil in her hand, sending it rolling across the desktop. Stepping forward, he caught it right before it clattered to the floor.

"Oh, Mr. Travers! You scared me!" She tucked an errant curl behind her ear in a nervous gesture.

"I'm not sure why...This is my home, after all, which is why I'm surprised to find you still in it. Aren't you finished with the lesson?" He looked around as if searching for her missing pupils.

"Yes, we're done for the day, and Peter was a marvelous helper, by the way," she said and accepted the offered pencil from him. "I know I should've left with the children, but it was so quiet...I thought I could work in peace."

A blank look formed on his face. "Don't you work at a library?" By definition it should embody both of those things — peace and quiet.

"That's true, but I can't write if I'm working. And since Mr. Kilney has given me extra time in the afternoons for these lessons, I thought I'd take advantage..." She trailed off, shaking her head with a short laugh. "Never mind, it was silly of me. I'll pack my things and head home. I apologize for the inconvenience."

"I didn't say you had to go." He dragged one of the chairs up to her desk, so they faced each other. Warning bells sounded in his head. *What are you doing? You're trying to avoid spending time alone with this woman!*

"I don't?"

"No, not as long as you answer my questions." He didn't know where the ultimatum came from, but the idea of discovering some of her secrets grew on him.

Frowning, she asked, "What sorts of questions?"

"Nothing sordid. Just your usual run-of-the-mill inquiry like why'd you come to Manchester? Why leave your family in Hampshire?" He knew a little about her sisters and the country sounded idyllic after his upbringing in the rookery. Yet she'd chosen to leave.

"I needed to get away — strike out on my own. The library position allows me that kind of freedom and opportunity."

"They didn't have something for you in the village? Or a closer town? Manchester is quite the change." He refused to ask about potential suitors, not wanting to imagine the type of man she'd end up with, certainly not a criminal like him, despite the kiss they'd stolen.

"Mr. Kilney was a friend of my father. It seemed like the logical choice to work for him instead of a stranger. Besides, the library's perfect for..." The sentence broke off, and she brought a hand to her lips as if she hadn't intended to reveal that next bit of information.

"Perfect for what?" Intrigued, he dropped his elbows to his knees and leaned forward. Perhaps this was the real reason she was here; he knew there had to be more behind her story to compel such drastic action. "Does it have to do with whatever's happening there?" He motioned to the messy writing in front of her.

Smoothing a hand over the cream paper, she nodded. "I'm writing a children's book, and the library provides the room and research I need. And while it's not London, I thought the smaller publishers here would be more inclined to accept a manuscript from a woman," she said, a blush staining her cheeks, though the defiance in her tone belied any embarrassment.

"What sort of children's book?" Curiosity filled him at her ambitious notion. He didn't doubt her talent if her passion for the books she read to the children was anything to go by. He figured it wasn't too much of a leap to create her own stories. But it was bizarre that she'd want to go into a profession along with her job at the library. Women didn't do such things, at least not women of her blood. Though she wasn't noble, she was still a gently-bred lady who didn't need to work to survive unlike the women of his acquaintance in Devil's Haven. And she wanted not one but two jobs! What about marriage and a family?

She clearly loved children, and he couldn't imagine her never having a babe of her own. Unbidden, a vision of her full with his child rose in his mind.

Are you mad?

Shaking his head, he quickly dispelled the ridiculous idea.

"It's about a fairy who needs to reclaim a family heirloom in order to restore the balance in their kingdom. She's helped by intelligent woodland creatures along the way." Excitement sparkled in her eyes as she summarized the plot giving her a glow that he itched to near and touch. *You must resist.*

"Well, that sounds interesting," he said instead. A weak substitute in his mind.

She laughed. "It's meant for children. You don't have to feign interest, though I appreciate the effort." Shifting to her feet, she stacked the papers and tucked them into her satchel before rounding the desk. Sunlight from the window glinted off her blonde curls creating a halo effect that took his breath away.

"I wouldn't lie about such a thing." He took a step into her path causing her to stop short and stare up at him, wariness and curiosity warring within the blue irises.

"Mr. Travers…"

"Jonathan," he said out of reflex, needing to hear her say his name.

"Then you must agree to call me Hazel."

"Done." To seal the promise, he finally gave in to the desire he'd been fighting all afternoon. Hell, what he'd been fighting for longer than that if he were honest and kissed her. Cupping her face with both hands like the precious gem he feared she was becoming to him, he peppered gentle kisses over her mouth, drawing on her plump bottom lip until she sighed in acquiescence. She tasted of summer — fresh and sweet with heat enough to burn him. And for a moment, all his worries and alarms calmed, whisked away by a midsummer breeze that heralded the sudden rush of a rainstorm.

"Jonathan..." she whispered as they separated for a breath, her lashes fluttering against flushed cheeks. His heartbeat faltered — such a simple utterance, yet it pierced him.

Their tongues intertwined again, and the probing kiss flared into a blaze as her taste tempted and coaxed. He thought he could stand there indefinitely, wrapped up in her, but of course, it wasn't meant to be.

Swishing footsteps outside signaled Mrs. Wilson tidying up in the hallway and served as a cold splash of water on his head. Reluctantly, he released Hazel, letting his hands drop and thrusting them in his pockets so he wouldn't reach for her again.

"I didn't mean for things to escalate, but it seems I have a hard time controlling myself around you," he admitted, trying to gauge her reaction.

"Really? I wouldn't have guessed. You have a remarkably good poker face at times." A shy smile beamed at him as she placed a comforting hand on his arm and squeezed. "I'll let myself out, but I will see you Tuesday. Won't I, Jonathan?"

He inwardly groaned. Yes, she would dammit.

"Oh!" She halted in the doorway to look back. "I forgot to ask, but our talk of my writing and work reminds me. What exactly do you do working such erratic hours?"

The imaginary cold water from earlier turned to ice as his chance to finally scare her away from him appeared. "I'm part of the Cobblewallers Gang. A criminal who collects debts of money or blood if the funds aren't available."

"I see." The muted tone of her voice revealed nothing. He expected revulsion, shock, yet she displayed nothing resembling what he thought a lady should when it came to him and Devil's Haven. "Good day, Jonathan."

He stood stunned at the abrupt farewell. Confusion pounded at the back of his head, but there was nothing to be done for it until Tuesday if she decided to return or not.

Jonathan didn't know which he hoped for more.

CHAPTER NINE

A small bronze plaque proclaiming Black Press graced the front of the brick building as Hazel studied the publishing house before crossing the busy street. After speaking about her book with Jonathan yesterday, it made her realize she needed to start making connections with potential publishers.

And perhaps it'll get your mind off that spontaneous kiss and shocking revelation.

He'd surprised her with the kiss, but she couldn't say she regretted the move. In fact, it only made her more eager to explore that side of their...friendship? Relationship? The correct term for their bond escaped her, but whatever they were made her heart pound and silly daydreams to take over her mind whether working at the library or in her room trying to write.

But his current employment concerned her. A member of a notorious gang? She'd heard the rumblings between the children, and Dot had mentioned something about them, too. Though, Jonathan didn't exhibit any outward behaviors she would attribute to such a criminal. *And how many of those do you know to judge him by?*

Images of the boarding house cropped up, and she reasoned that it seemed he was trying to better himself — to leave that lifestyle behind. Could she really criticize the path he'd taken to survive? Surely, growing up in the rookery held its own sorts of challenges, but he'd navigated them best he could even now while tending to his brother.

"Coming or going, miss?" A man stood in the company doorway waiting for her to enter, and she locked thoughts of Jonathan away for the time being.

Remember what you're here for.

"Coming, thank you." She strode forward with a purposeful step and gathered all of her courage. Today, she'd show the beginning chapters of her manuscript to someone with the power to publish it to the masses. Nerves and elation added buoyancy to her steps. Ever since she'd discovered storytelling, her life had been building to this moment when she could reach her goal of becoming a published author like her idol: Lewis Carroll.

As she crossed the threshold, the sound of the printing press and the smell of ink overwhelmed her senses. A man sat at a desk to the left of her, furiously scribbling in a ledger, as she approached.

"Good afternoon, sir. Would you happen to be Mr. Black?" she asked, gripping the pages of her manuscript tightly in slick palms.

The man glanced up, dropped his gaze to her side, then dismissed her. "We're not accepting any queries at this time."

Her hopeful smile dimmed a little, but she pressed on. "I see...Would it be possible for you to read over my story to keep in mind for the future? It's a wonderful tale for children full of illustrations and — "

"I'm afraid not." The man, Mr. Henley, according to a placard which lay practically hidden behind a tower of papers, set the pen down and folded his hands in front of him. "We have stacks..." Meeting her gaze, he gestured to the aforementioned pile. "...of manuscripts to get through for potential distribution. And by names we recognize a sight more than yours. Who did you say you were?"

"Miss Hazel Taylor. And I understand your dilemma, however, I think you'll find..."

He held up a staying hand. "The answer is no. I wish you the best of luck, although I doubt there are many publishing houses searching for a children's book written by an unknown woman at this time." With that firm prediction hanging in the air, he picked up his pen and continued working.

Hazel held her story closer as if to shield herself from the potential truth of his words. Turning on her heel, she hurried outside and took a scant number of steps before spying an alleyway to duck into. Brick met her back, a stinging chill seeping through the cotton of her dress. Strained breaths filled her lungs as she closed her eyes and focused on the cold. It provided some much-needed distance between her and the discouraging encounter.

You'll be all right; this is only the first publisher you've visited.

Yet, his foreboding words that no one would be interested rang in her ears as her sisters' doubts came crashing around her. She couldn't let them be right. Couldn't fail.

Throat tightening, her chest constricted, and she rubbed the area over her heart. *No, not here.* Sweat dampened the back of her neck as the memory of being pinned to the ground after the accident flashed in her mind. The rough carnage of the carriage digging into her skin.

I survived. Mama and Papa are dead.

Fate saved her for a reason; she couldn't disappoint. She pictured holding a bound version of her story, imagined becoming a child's favorite author, and after a few minutes, the impending attack morphed into a welcome numbness.

Everything would work out. She'd take it one day at a time, and eventually, someone would accept her manuscript. Pushing away from the wall, Hazel straightened her shoulders, a determined glint in her eyes, and stepped back out into the milling crowd on the sidewalk and headed home.

She knew her work was worth publishing — children would love it — and that belief was all she needed to continue.

Unfortunately, that optimism was short-lived, and by nightfall, doubts ate at her. What did she think she was doing? Why did she think she was capable of such a feat? That anyone would want to read her stories?

A girl from the country who'd never even left the village she grew up in until a month ago. What did she have to offer?

Most of the time she shoved aside self-doubt and pushed forward, but days like today made her feel like she could never live up to the level of Carroll, Austen, or Verne. They had experience and wells of creativity along with the talent of crafting something beyond the mundane she feared her own writing encompassed.

Wiping a salty tear away, she stared down at the latest piece she'd written. The words ran together into a flat, boring mess until she snatched the page up from the desk and crumpled it before tossing it to the floor. Why was it so difficult for her to put her ideas to paper?

A whole colorful world thrived inside her imagination. She could see the smallest details of her characters, yet when it came to writing them down, everything seemed to fall apart. Sighing in dejection, she put away her writing materials; she would get no further tonight with the mood she was in.

Hazel blew out the lone candle she'd been using for light and crawled into bed, lying flat on her back, and staring out the window to the moonless sky. Hopefully, she would dream and tomorrow be in better spirits — prepared to continue writing instead of succumbing to the melancholy of tonight.

Her survival couldn't be in vain. If her parents were alive, she held no doubts they would've published dozens of papers by now and educated people the world over. Yet, writing a simple children's book eluded her.

Taking a labored breath, silent tears trailed down her cheeks at the failure.

Be better, Hazel. You have to make this work.

WEEKS PASSED SINCE her rejection and the first lesson with Mary and Lizzie, and their small group had grown in size. Apparently, news traveled quickly about the lessons and none of the children wanted to be left out. Most of their time together these days consisted less of her reading solo and more of everyone trying their hand at a word or sentence.

While not her original purpose for coming to Devil's Haven, she figured it didn't hurt. If she kept an optimistic attitude, perhaps she was tutoring the very children who would read her book when it was published. So, really, everyone benefited.

Well, almost everyone.

She didn't know what Jonathan gained from all of this past his brother being occupied, but perhaps that was enough. Shrugging at the conundrum, Hazel collected her things after the lesson and moved to join Jonathan in a third-story room where he was stripping the tattered wallpaper before painting. Moving to a corner out of the way, she pulled out the sketches she'd been working on and her box of watercolors.

"You'd be more comfortable downstairs with the desk and chair than sitting on the floor," Jonathan said as he paused his work

"It's easier for me to see the sequence of the story if I lay everything out. Besides, I'd rather spend time with you than downstairs alone. If I wanted that, I'd return home."

He sighed at her stubbornness but didn't push. "Suit yourself."

She'd taken to spending longer periods of time with him once the children left to work on her story. Another prayer of thanks filled her after Mr. Kilney had agreed to extend her break again as long as she made up the time in the evening. How fortunate that Dot's clergyman father endorsed her visits to Devil's Haven, and Mr. Kilney didn't want to get on the wrong side of God.

And lucky for her that Jonathan didn't back up his protesting of longer visits by kicking her out. Especially after her first return upon learning how he spent the majority of his days. He'd tried explaining why it wasn't a good idea for her to be alone with him, voicing valid points, but like she thought before, her perception of danger was skewed. Along with any care for propriety.

Growing up in Hampshire, the Taylor family stuck out like a sore thumb with their varied intellectual pursuits and wild natures. Her mother aided Papa's research in the gardens instead of participating in women's quilting circles. And Lily's scandal with a stable boy confirmed their lowered status. Concerning herself with propriety now seemed superfluous. Though, she didn't plan on completely ruining her reputation.

Does one ever plan such a thing?

Returning to her story, Hazel glanced over the pencil sketches, switching scenes to create a better flow, and mapping out in her mind what would come next. Once satisfied, she started filling in the colors of one of the character sketches. With her skirt surrounding her, she carefully leaned forward and applied a brush of orange to Tom, the fox. The quiet sweeping sound of her brushstrokes mixed with the tearing of old wallpaper from Jonathan as they worked in companionable silence.

A calm sense of contentment carried her away as she drifted further into her imagination. For some reason, she found it easier to concentrate here in the middle of the rookery with Jonathan than in the peaceful library. Perhaps it was the fear of Mr. Kilney looking over her shoulder.

"What do you think about adding a blackboard to the classroom?"

Hazel jerked in surprise before looking up from her station on the floor to see Jonathan running a slow hand over one of the stripped walls. He studied the empty space as if imagining the identical room downstairs.

"It would help me show the children their letters, but where would we get something like that?" Since she'd started the lessons, it had become clear how ill-equipped she was. One by one, she had to walk to each child and reiterate the same lesson multiple times. A blackboard would reduce the monotonous task significantly.

"You don't need to concern yourself with the specifics. I'll take care of it. I just wanted to make sure it was something you thought you'd need," he said. Pulling a scrap of paper he kept in his back pocket for notes, he scratched a line across the sheet before shoving it back in place and starting to measure the wall.

Hazel watched him for a moment more, admiring his dedication to getting things right. *Not to mention his form*, she thought with a faint smile. Stocky and handsome, he imbued the rough and tumble look of the rookery, but it drew her in, nonetheless. The men in Hampshire were of a similar musculature due to their work on the farms dotting the countryside, but theirs was a wholesome almost innocent strength. There was nothing innocent about Jonathan. He possessed a hardened edge which could only be gained through harsher circumstances.

Turning back to her own work, Hazel sketched out an idea she'd been toying with since meeting Jonathan. A battered badger with a heart of gold; it would be something to reflect what she saw in him. She didn't know how he'd feel about inspiring one of her characters — her sisters certainly hadn't always appreciated it — but it felt right to include him when he'd been such a good friend to her.

More than a friend.

Quickly, a black badger with a light brown streak came to life, and she held the sketch up to the light streaming in through the front window. A roguish twinkle glittered in the badger's eyes echoing its human counterpart, and she set it aside with the rest of the animal sketches, proud of the finished product.

"You know, a blackboard won't do us much good if the children don't have their own individual slates." Jonathan's musing brought her head back up. He'd moved to lean against the wall with his arms and legs crossed as he watched her. She'd caught him in the act a few times — watching her write and draw. At first it made her nervous, afraid of embarrassing herself, but then she thought it was flattering. If he had trouble keeping his gaze to himself, who was she to stop him?

"That's true," she drawled. "And I suppose you'd take care of that as well?"

"Naturally." He grinned, revealing the endearing crooked tooth near the front of his mouth, a remnant of a stray punch, no doubt.

"At this rate, we might have to start calling our reading room: Travers's School for Children." His smile faltered before green eyes narrowed in a heated stare. The change confused her until she realized what she'd said. *Travers's School for Children.* It sounded like she'd included herself in the naming as if they were a happily married couple intent on teaching the children of Devil's Haven. Which was ridiculous, of course.

Jonathan wasn't interested in marriage, and she didn't want to be a schoolteacher. While she admired her father's profession, she was meant to be an author; she felt it in her bones. Yet, a vision of what their future could be formed in her mind's eye. Married to a husband as supportive and passionate as Jonathan. Welcoming the children into the classroom and providing a fun educational experience instead of the strict regimen they had now with Miss Crenshaw.

But that's not for me.

Shoving the daydream away, she tried to skim over the implication. "I mean you've provided this room where we can safely meet. And now you're offering to provide school supplies. You're a regular headmaster."

"I do like the sound of *headmaster* when it comes from your lips." His low, suggestive tone sent a shiver down her back and sparks rose within her body. It'd been weeks since their last impromptu kiss. *Entirely too long.* She'd started to wonder if their two joinings had been flukes to satisfy an inquisitive part of Jonathan instead of true interest on his part.

"You have unusual reactions to the most innocent of words."

"Sunshine, nothing you say ever sounds innocent to a rogue like me," he said, dropping his crossed arms and walking closer. "If you only knew the thoughts I have about you constantly running around in my head. Then you'd be running straight back to your safe library."

"I think we both know there's nothing you could do that would scare me off." She trusted him, even after he told her more about his past with the Cobblewallers Gang and his boss, Lucien. *What an enlightening conversation that had been.* All that mattered was that he wanted to change, and he backed the resolve with action.

"I suppose you're right. You've overlooked my current employment. Ignored the fact that you were attacked before I could —"

"Don't," she said, standing up and bracing a hand on his chest, feeling his steady heartbeat underneath the linen cloth. He never wore a jacket or vest when they were together — only the one layer of clothing, relaxed and casual. "You couldn't have known what was going to happen. You didn't even know me then, not really. I was just the woman volunteering to read to your brother."

His calloused palm covered hers, a thumb stroking over a blue vein. "I knew it wasn't safe for you. That it was only a matter of time before —"

She cut him off with a swift, hard kiss to his mouth — taking charge of what she wanted and quieting his distress, though his concern melted her admittedly soft heart. He was so protective, and his protection didn't only extend to her. She'd seen the way he cared for Peter and the children. Making sure they were fed if hungry. Calling Dr. Forrester for a visit if one got injured. It surprised her that he had such strong caretaker tendencies considering his own upbringing wasn't the most loving from what she'd gathered from Peter. Yet, he'd diverged from the path of his father and mother before him.

"It's not your fault; it's not mine. Those men bear the responsibility. Let's leave it behind," she whispered. They hadn't mentioned that day in all their time together, and she didn't want to dredge it up now. An unspoken debate passed between their gazes: hers imploring and his, eventually, resigned to her request.

"If that's what you want."

"It is."

"Then I suppose I must abide by it," he said and swept another hand over her cheek before stroking the wild curl dangling by her neck.

Deciding to lighten the mood, she joked. "And here I thought you were going to be headmaster, but it looks like I'm in charge."

A rueful chuckle bubbled up between them. "You have no idea."

CHAPTER TEN

"So, if not headmaster, I suppose *landlord* would be more apt?" Hazel asked, twirling away with a playful push. "Since you're fixing this up to be a boarding house?"

"If I ever finish which is debatable at this point," he said as he tracked her across the room, still reeling from her unexpected kiss, recalling the way she'd pressed her mouth to his. How to continue with such a mundane turn of the conversation? A topic that already occupied most of his time, tormenting him.

Two years had passed since he'd started this journey, and while the building showed progress, he worried it'd never reach the place he wanted it to be for actual residents.

"You'll finish. What made you decide to pursue such a project? It sounds very noble — all of the safety precautions you're taking, according to Peter."

"Don't start thinking I'm some kind of saint. That's just good business. Devil's Haven lacks adequate housing for everyone; I'm just taking advantage of a need."

"I don't believe that," Hazel said, blonde brows crinkling.

"Well, you still don't believe it's dangerous for you to be traipsing around the rookery, so I can't say I'm surprised. You see the best in things even when there's evidence to the contrary." *Case in point? Me.*

"You make me seem like a child."

"I think we both know that's not how I see you, but you do exude a certain optimistic charm. Face it, sunshine, you're an innocent — unjaded by the world yet."

"Don't be so sure..." An inscrutable look passed over her face before disappearing and her usual bright smile popped up. "When will you finish? No doubt people are excited to move in. You've done a wonderful job so far."

"And you didn't even see it in the beginning," he said. An image of how rundown the building used to be sprang to mind. "The timeline's up in the air. I need to be sure I have enough capital to cover any problems that come up."

An issue he hadn't worried about when he'd planned to continue working for Lucien.

Her forehead furrowed at his explanation. "How will you know when you have enough? And with your skills, I think you'd be able to handle most issues yourself."

Her faith in him sent a rush of pride pulsing through his blood, even if it was unwarranted. "I'd rather be safe than sorry. This will all be for nothing if I go under before really getting started."

"Jonathan, I understand your fear, but trust me, you can do this. You will succeed." A sincere smile formed on her face.

"How can you believe that?" He paced across the room, running a hand through his hair in frustration. "I don't deserve your faith or trust."

"Nonsense!" Following his path, she stopped him in his tracks with a hand to his arm as he met her determined blue eyes. "You've proven you're worthy of all of those things. You're a good brother. A strong protector. A good man, Jonathan Travers."

An unfamiliar feeling overwhelmed him at Hazel's passionate defense. No one had ever believed in him like she did, and it excited as well as disturbed him. What would happen when he inevitably let her down?

Unwilling to consider the possibility, he pulled her closer, needing to mask the emotions bombarding him with the one thing he was willing to accept: the desire she evoked from him. And their earlier kiss hadn't been enough to satisfy it by far.

Why not give in to his selfish needs?

It wouldn't be the first time. An image of his father approaching him for money to rent a new flat impeded on the moment before he slammed the door shut on those memories.

I'm changing. I'm not the same greedy bastard.

With an arm around Hazel's waist, he shifted them until she leaned against the desk, perfectly positioned for his attentions. Despite misgivings, it appeared she didn't share the same apprehension, and who was he to deny them something they both wanted?

Hazel's arms wrapped around his neck in eagerness. He loved how guileless she was. She enjoyed physical intimacy and wasn't afraid to show it, even if it did put her reputation at risk if they were ever caught. Another shiver of concern scraped along his nerves at the thought of any harm coming to her.

We're careful. You can have this one moment.

Each time their lips met, it felt hotter and more intense, building towards a culmination he knew could never happen.

"Jonathan..."

No one used his full name. It was always Jon or Jonny, but he loved hearing it uttered from her lips. Letting his mouth drift over a downy cheek before lowering to her neck, he cupped a generous breast through the fabric of her dress. What he wouldn't give for a taste of that bounty.

And what's stopping you?

The wicked idea floated in like the smoke of an opium den — sweet and decadent. And he thought, *What the hell?* They'd come this far, and she'd never protested, perhaps he would be lucky again. *Or you scare her off for good...*

Kisses on lips were one thing. Kisses on sensitive nipples were an entirely different matter. But resistance was futile.

Scattering light pecks over her neck, Jonathan slipped one button from its mooring and waited for her reaction. When Hazel remained quiet, he continued his task until the blue cotton gaped open to reveal a white chemise and corset, her breasts offered up to him like two ripe peaches.

Daring to meet her gaze to ascertain her feelings, he saw the desire as her pupils eclipsed the midnight blue irises. "How are you doing, sunshine?"

In a surprisingly bold move, she moved his hand to cup her through the thin barrier, so he could stroke the budding nipple underneath. "Does this answer your question?" The husky tone in her voice drove his hunger higher.

Message fucking received.

Bending his head, he nipped at her before tugging the lace-edged neckline down and sucking hard on the berry tip, eliciting a sharp gasp from Hazel. Like a starving beast, he devoured her supple flesh, switching between breasts until they were splotched red from the rasp of his beard.

"You know how sweet you taste?" He whispered the illicit question in her delicate ear. "Like a freshly picked fruit on a spring morning. You're a damn feast of delights, and I can't wait to sample your cream." He couldn't resist voicing one of his deepest desires: to lick between her thighs as she came on his tongue. Completely inappropriate. *Yet necessary.*

She shuddered at his words. "What does that mean? Because I think I'd like that." Her innocent question dropped like a brick on his distracted head, reminding him once again that she wasn't one of the women on the corner. She didn't know what she was doing no matter her eagerness to learn. But he knew better than to mess around with a virgin.

Damn these conflicting emotions! They were tearing him apart inside.

Resolved to end this interlude, he began putting her back to rights, rebuttoning the row of brown beads as if they were on fire, before stepping back. "Never mind that. I shouldn't have said anything. It's time for you to head back."

"Tell me what you meant." Hazel tried reaching for his arm, but he retreated further away. If she touched him again, they'd be right back where they started.

"It's not fit for a lady's ears."

"Neither is having a man's mouth suckling my..." Alarmed, he covered her mouth before she finished the sentence, the filthy words coming from her inciting his desire even more, proving his depravity.

"Don't say it." Sighing, he released her again. "See what a bad influence I am? Compromising you? You don't even know what you're asking, but I guarantee it's more than you can give. More proof that we don't suit."

"That's not true. None of it. And you're an educational influence."

That drew a harsh laugh from him. He doubted anyone had ever described him as educational.

"Nevertheless, it's time we returned you to where you belong."

Her mouth firmed in a straight line. "I'm beginning to tire of your hot and cold nature." Fire danced in her gaze as small fists formed at her sides, and Jonathan braced for theatrics. "You kiss me but push me away a moment later. Insisting on denying us something we both clearly want when I've told you time and again: I'm a grown woman who can look after herself. I know my mind and my limits."

"You've experienced the barest hint of carnal lust yet believe you're an expert. Trust you can handle the furthest extent of my desire, but you're wrong." He clenched his own tight fists, desperate to make her understand. "I wish you'd tire of me. Tire of the whole goddamned Devil's Haven. Maybe then these blasted emotions of possession and need wouldn't plague me, and I could return to the life I had before you burst into it."

A pale expression of hurt darkened her features before she turned to face the window looking out on the street. "My apologies for making these past weeks so difficult for you. You've been generous despite wishing me gone, and I've pushed and bullied for more. Adding to your troubles."

"Ah, hell..." Jonathan hated hearing the sadness in her tone, loathed that he'd upset her. But she turned him inside out. He didn't know how to control these emotions around her. "Sunshine, you don't need to apologize. What you're doing for the children is kindhearted and good, and I don't regret my decision to give you the room."

Moving to stand behind her, he dropped a tender kiss to her shoulder before resting his forehead on the gentle curve. "That's the problem," he whispered. "I don't regret any of our time together, and my desire for you rages like the furnaces in the factories. But we can't give into passion. It would ruin you, and a rookery life with a soon to be ex-gang member isn't in your future."

An ache cracked in his chest at the admission.

Hazel's hand reached backward to envelop his in a comforting squeeze. "Let me be the judge of that. It may have escaped your notice, but I'm quite an unusual woman. Ask anyone back home. Whatever's between us doesn't scare me even if it's only meant to be temporary."

A wisp of amusement punctured some of his misery. Nothing about her escaped his notice including what a unique treasure she was.

"You don't have to answer now, but please think about it." Hazel shifted to run the back of her hand along his cheek before gathering her things to leave. They followed their usual ritual of him walking her to the door in silence, and the secret guard he'd hired to watch her safely home emerged on the other side of the street.

Hazel wanted him to contemplate ruining her. Taking her to his bed and stealing her virginity for himself.

Peculiar, naive woman.

But possibly his woman?

CHAPTER ELEVEN

"**A** letter for you, miss."

A maid placed the missive next to Hazel where she lounged in the Kilney drawing room with Elizabeth Gaskell's *North and South* — needing a comfort read after the argument with Jonathan. During the walk home yesterday, her body tingled from their kisses and his brusque words. The emotional exchange roused another attack, forcing her to beg off from her shift at the library in an attempt to calm her nerves in private.

And here she was the next morning still trying to combat the chaotic feeling by reading one of her favorite books — attempting to focus her thoughts on Mr. Thornton rather than constricting lungs and heart.

Thanking the girl, Hazel traded her book for the small rectangle of paper sealed with her family's initials. *Perhaps you should wait until you've calmed more...*

Recognizing the neat handwriting as her sister Caraway's, another barrage of pointed questions and doubts about her decisions didn't seem like the best way to achieve a state of relaxation.

Deal with it head-on, so you don't have to dwell on it.

Resigned, Hazel broke the seal, and upon reaching the familiar "Your loving sister" valediction at the end, her predictions proved true along with the added admonishment for not responding in a timely manner. Was it any wonder she didn't reply? How many times must she reiterate her ability to care for herself?

Except when it comes to the risks you're taking with your reputation.

But she silenced that voice which sounded annoyingly like her eldest sister. As an independent woman, it was her right to choose how she spent her time and with whom. It may not be the accepted way of society, but her family had long ago disappointed those expectations. She saw no reason to heed them now.

Setting the letter aside, she rested her head against the velvet cushioning of the chair and took deep breaths. Bluebirds surrounded her as Mrs. Kilney adored them and had the room made up with all things ornithological. Hazel could only imagine the woman's reaction to viewing the real thing in Hampshire. She smiled at the thought as her gaze moved from the wallpaper to framed oil paintings until they settled on the tiny stuffed birds in iron cages resting on the mantle.

A frown distorted her features. Kinship with the trapped knick-knacks beat in her chest — constraints placed on her by her family, the Kilneys, society. The only time she truly felt free of judgement was in Devil's Haven with Jonathan. He never made her feel less than or incapable even when he worried about her safety.

Aside from our dispute.

It was less about control and doubt and more about protection. He trusted her intelligence, believed in her dream. Indeed, his active support was undeniable.

I chose correctly.

For if she'd searched for someone to love, a better man could not have been found than Jonathan Travers.

Don't be ridiculous. You don't love the man. You just have a strong affinity for him.

A sharp knock broke her contemplation, and Greyston announced the unexpected arrival of Dot who glided gracefully into the room on padded slippers. Struggling to her feet within the volume of skirts, Hazel accepted Dot's brief hug before taking their seats, Dot pulling at the brown leather of her gloves and packing them in her reticule.

"How are you, dear? I feel like it's been ages since we last spoke," she said with a huff, curiosity burning in her eyes.

"It's certainly been eventful since our last visit." Hazel replayed the changes and wondered where to begin, but it seemed like Dot had her own agenda to follow as she launched her first question.

"Last I heard, you planned on returning to Devil's Haven, and now my father's mentioned seeing two men carry a large blackboard into the Travers home. You wouldn't happen to know anything about that would you?"

"Ah, yes...It would seem that I've become something of a tutor." Hazel shrugged and played with one of the buttons on her dress as a distraction.

"A tutor? Of what? For whom?" Putting Hazel in mind of a conquistador of the Spanish Inquisition, Dot shot query after query like cannon fire.

"The children, of course. Someone asked if I could teach her to read, and it snowballed from there. It's not like I planned for the transition. I have enough on my plate as is." Her unfinished manuscript haunted her from upstairs. Even though she used time after lessons to write, more often than not she ended up talking with Jonathan or concocting new lessons.

"But you enjoy it?"

"Well, yes, but that doesn't change the fact that it's not the reason I came to Manchester. Volunteering was meant to be part of charity, and selfishly, perhaps research into what young minds want to read," she said exasperatedly. She hadn't voiced this frustration to Jonathan because she *did* love the children and seeing the light of understanding dawn in their eyes, but what about her personal ambitions?

Is there room for both?

"I understand, but could this mean your life should take a different path?" Dot's gentle voice matched the commiseration in her eyes. She knew it wasn't what Hazel wanted to hear.

"You think I should give up the idea of becoming an author? I thought you liked what you've read so far." She'd shared a few chapters here and there for feedback, and positive encouragement had always been Dot's response. Could it have been a lie? A friend being cautious with her feelings?

"No, that's not what I'm saying, and of course, I loved your story. But you can be meant for more than one thing in life, right? Focusing on one doesn't mean giving up the other — just putting it on hold until later. For the right time," Dot clarified.

Hazel didn't know how to explain that she'd been doing that for years already. This was her taking charge and making it the right time. She'd waited and dreamed and waited some more, then her parents died and she almost did, too. The time for putting things off was over. But that was too much to discuss over an afternoon visit, and frankly, she didn't want to dive into that conversation anyway.

So, instead, she pasted on a smile and agreed. "You may be right. I suppose only time will tell where I'll end up: a teacher or an author or both."

But dividing her attention — officially — between the two positions felt like admitting defeat. The reading lessons must remain in the volunteering realm while she concentrated on writing. Becoming an author was her one constant, the glue holding everything together in her life as silly as it may seem to outsiders.

Dot sighed with relief, her shoulders drooping as she leaned back. "I'm happy to hear you're open to the possibilities. Now, tell me about Mr. Travers..."

Another potential battlefield.

Seeing as Dot was a clergyman's daughter, Hazel doubted she'd approve of the physical intimacies she and Jonathan had exchanged thus far. She hated lying to her friend even by omission, but she couldn't risk tales of her actions getting back to Dot's father then Mr. Kilney. It would jeopardize everything.

Lifting her hands in a nonchalant gesture, she shared tidbits of their meetings but ultimately intimated that they hardly spoke with one another, and that Mrs. Wilson was her main source of contact.

After all, a female chaperone, however informal, kept up appearances of propriety. If Hazel couldn't care less about such a thing, Dot might, and her good opinion mattered.

CHAPTER TWELVE

"I'm stepping down soon. You should start thinking of my replacement," Jonathan said after asking Max to leave him and Lucien alone for a moment. The words had been brewing inside him for a while, and after the stunt Lucien pulled with Abbott, it was time to spit them out or give up on his plan. As he inched closer to finishing the building renovations, and with Hazel's support, now was as good a time as any to start distancing himself from Lucien.

"This again? I thought we'd settled the matter." Lucien sat back with his hands laced over his portly stomach, a shrewd look in his eye.

"Hardly. You know I've been working on opening new housing for Devil's Haven. And with Pete in my care, he and the project will need to become my priorities." Jonathan stood tall and confident; he wasn't afraid of Lucien. But he did worry about the man refusing to relinquish his control and acting out against Pete or even Hazel. It wouldn't surprise him if Lucien kept tabs on his personal life to use as leverage.

"An admirable job you're doing there, but I fail to see how that's my problem. You work for me until I decide to let you go. You've been working on this side project for what? Two years now?" Lucien scratched his chin. "Doesn't seem like you're making much progress, and haven't I been generous in my support? Who helped you buy the building in the first place? And this is how you want to repay me?"

Jonathan knew the topic of purchase would come up eventually. He regretted ever approaching Lucien for help. At the time, he'd been desperate to increase his lot in life. He hadn't had the kind of connections needed to make such a purchase, and he appreciated Lucien's tacit approval — branching out beyond the Cobblewallers to diversify his funds.

How wrong he'd been. Lucien made sure to keep him busy collecting debts which slowed his ability to do the majority of the manual labor for renovations himself. The longer it took him to open the boarding house the tighter he felt Lucien's hold.

"You see my dilemma. I haven't made enough progress because I've been occupied working for you. And while I appreciate the aid you've given me," Jonathan resisted a snort of derision. "It's time I struck out on my own. Surely, you understand that sentiment as a self-made man yourself."

He hoped appealing to Lucien's ego would further his cause, though the man's expression hadn't thawed yet. Raucous laughter outside the office filtered through the closed door — a light-hearted atmosphere attempting to break the tension consuming the room.

"You're still a pup. You've got a lot to learn if you think you're ready to handle such an undertaking as becoming a full-time landlord to the poor bastards of Devil's Haven." Standing to his full height which put him at Jonathan's shoulders, Lucien looked down at the gold pocket watch hanging from his tweed vest. "I'm afraid I have another engagement to attend to, but my answer stands. You're too valuable for me to let you go off on some hare-brained scheme. I've indulged your little hobby as it hasn't interfered with your work, with our plans for the future. But now it's threatening to; see that it doesn't."

Dictate handed down like a tiny god, he walked to the door and ushered Jonathan out in front of him before locking the door.

"You can't expect me to work for you forever," Jonathan said.

"And why not? You've known for years you'll be the one to take my place when I'm dead and buried. This is just a hiccup in the road, and I've said all I have to say on the matter. Now, why don't you join the rest of the boys before you head out for the night rounds? Enjoy a drink and one of the whores. Plenty to go around."

Jonathan watched as Lucien waddled down the hallway to the main part of the gambling den before turning to leave out the back door. He'd stayed once before, years ago. *Never again*. The stench of smoke and sex had clung to him long after leaving, and the thought of experiencing it again after knowing the sweetness of Hazel made his stomach revolt.

Stepping into the foggy alleyway, he tried to figure out what to do if Lucien proved serious in his threat to keep Jonathan tied to him indefinitely. Not many men left Lucien's gang and lived to tell the tale. Another truth he knew intimately as he'd once been one of the men to silence such deserters. But he was smart; he could puzzle out how to get out of this mess without its dangerous tendrils touching his family.

Even if he still wanted to remain in the crime lord's employ like his original plan, it'd be impossible once he started renting out flats. What if one of the residents became Lucien's debtor? He couldn't very well intimidate his own tenant out of their earnings.

What a hellish nightmare.

"How'd he take it?" Max asked from his position standing against the alley wall.

"Not well as expected. Expressed doubts that I'd even get the venture off the ground, but if I did, I'd still need to fulfill my duties to him." They exited the alley to walk side by side down the quiet street, heading towards their first mark of the evening. The freezing damp portended the coming winter, and Jonathan reveled in the icy chill. It numbed the strength of the storm bearing down on his future.

Max grunted. "Can't say I'm surprised; you knew that would be his answer."

"Doesn't mean I'm going to abide by it." He may have predicted Lucien's response, but tonight wasn't really about securing a safe exit from the Cobblewallers, although that would've made things a hell of a lot easier. No, he'd wanted to plant the seed that Jonathan's time with him neared its end. It was no longer a far off possibility.

"I wish you luck. You have my support," Max said as they reached the home of Abe Ellington, employee of Ashleigh Mills and debtor of seventy-five pounds. Jonathan nodded in appreciation. The men grew up together on these streets though their friendship hadn't always been easy. It eased his mind knowing someone backed him. Besides Hazel, of course.

"I appreciate it...Ready for another scintillating night of doing Lucien's dirty work?" he asked, pushing away all thoughts of his personal problems to concentrate on the task at hand. Max cracked his knuckles and grinned.

"Aren't I always?"

Knocking on the door, they waited as shuffling could be heard behind the door. Most people knew the score and transactions were completed within minutes; no one wanted to face him and Max. Though, every night one or two men decided they could evade the inevitable which usually ended with them bleeding on the floor from Max's fists. Jonathan hoped this would be one of the easy ones.

The door creaked open, and a hand motioned them inside. Wary, Jonathan took cautious steps followed by Max, their eyes trying to adjust to the pitch black of the home. Not a candle in sight, which didn't bode well — the back of his neck tingled with a strange awareness.

"Now!" Someone shouted as the door slammed shut and gas lanterns were lit, blinding him with the sudden light. A group of men tackled him and Max as shouting and cursing ensued. Wrestling an arm free, he threw a punch at one of the men holding him and managed to breach the grip as the man let go in pain. An arm wrapped around his neck, but Jonathan snapped his head back to hear the tell-tale crack of his assailant's nose and ducked under the loosened grasp.

Max roared as he smashed a boot in one man's gut, sending him careening into the kitchen table. Whipping around to face the men, Jonathan shouted, "Which one of you is Ellington? Come and fight like a man instead of hiding behind your friends."

A bald man ran towards him, answering the challenge. Twisting to the side, Jonathan caught Ellington's arm and fought him to the ground where he kneeled on his back and pulled the knife he kept in his boot. "All of you get out or else your friend gets a blade across the neck."

Everyone suspended further action except Max who shoved the man attacking him into the wall until he slumped to the ground unconscious. Raising an eyebrow, he asked, "Well? Wanting to see your friend dead? He said to get out!"

The men scrambled to exit like the cowards they were and left the three of them alone. Max motioned to Jonathan's chin, "You've got something there." As he rubbed the trickle of blood trailing down his own forehead.

Jonathan ignored his injury intent on dealing with Ellington. "What the hell do you think you're doing hosting an ambush for us? You think Lucien's out for you now; wait until he hears of this little gambit."

"Please, no! I'm sorry! I wasn't thinking! Please have mercy," the man begged — all bravado lost without the protection of his posse.

"Why should we when you tried to kill us?"

"Wasn't trying to kill, just warn you away until I have the money. Please, believe me! I was desperate." Jonathan held no doubts about that claim. Anyone willing to risk incurring Lucien's wrath courted ruin and death.

"Found it." Max held up a clinking coin purse hidden under an overturned bowl.

"Seems to me you have something for us, Ellington. Next time, skip the theatrics. That is...if Lucien doesn't come for retribution first." Jonathan threatened, although it made for bad business killing clients. Hard collecting money from a dead man. However, sometimes it became necessary to showcase what happens to dissenters.

The man shook as sobs drifted up to Jonathan's ears. Shaking his head in disgust, he pushed off the man and gestured to Max for them to take their leave. Clouds blocked the moonlight, but the darkness suited him fine.

"I know it's early, but do you want to call it a night? We can catch up tomorrow," Max said as he scrubbed at his jaw. Thankful for the suggestion, Jonathan agreed, and they parted ways. The only perk to working for Lucien were the irregular hours. As long as he got his money, he didn't bother to track their time.

It didn't take long for Jonathan to return to his room, though sleep would be impossible. His eye caught on the library book he still needed to return, and an idea sparked in his mind. Snatching it up, after double checking he wasn't bleeding anymore from his chin, he retraced his steps down the stairs and headed to the one place he should avoid but couldn't resist.

The Kilney Library. Hazel's home.

CHAPTER THIRTEEN

Jonathan stepped from the shadows and made his way to the library's back entrance. If he were smart, he'd wait until the next time he'd see Hazel again, but logic wasn't the pervading force riding him now. A restlessness jittered through his body, amplified by the energy expelled during the tussle. Dirt and scum filled his soul after dealing with the men earlier. He needed Hazel's sunshine to cleanse him.

Finding the door lock, he pulled out the small kit he'd brought for the occasion and quickly unlocked the latch, waiting a moment before pushing it slowly forward. Moonlight reached through the sliver of an opening to reveal the familiar storage room with shelves full of books and boxes — nothing changed since his last visit. The smell of parchment and ink permeated the small space as Jonathan stepped forward and made his way further into the empty building. Hazel lived upstairs in the home next door from what she'd mentioned to him, but there were connecting doors, so the Kilneys could pass between buildings. A clock struck two in the morning, and again he wondered at the stupidity of his actions.

What do you plan on doing? Watch her sleep? Wake her up? You'll probably scare the hell out of her.

One quick look to satisfy the yearning in his blood, then he'd leave with no one the wiser.

But as he neared the front of the library, he saw a light glowing on one of the side tables and Hazel hunched over her ever-present notebook. Blonde curls fell down her back, unbound and tantalizing his fingers with the image of tugging on the springy coils as he took her from behind. *That's not what you're here for.*

A high-pitched creak filled the room as his foot came down on an old floorboard. Hazel's shoulders tensed as she sat up, looking around. "Hello? Is somebody here?"

"It's just me, sunshine," he said, giving up the stealth act and moving into the ring of light that haloed her.

"Jonathan! What are you doing here? Are you all right?" She stood to greet him in disbelief, arms crossing over her chest, only a thin robe and nightgown hiding her body from him. He wondered if she noticed his dishevelment from the earlier fight.

"I thought I'd return this." He held up the borrowed book and stalked closer, hungry eyes devouring the sight of her so vulnerable and enticing.

"When did you get this?" Her brow wrinkled in confusion before her eyes widened. "Have you been here before? You weren't seen?" She leaned to the right to look over his shoulder as if someone would pop out like a gopher in spring.

"I'm alone, undetected, and it doesn't really matter how it landed in my possession, does it?" he asked, nervously scratching behind his ear. This was an awful idea. "I shouldn't have come. I don't know what I was thinking."

You weren't. At least not with your head.

He started backing away to get the hell out of there and prayed by morning she'd forget he'd ever shown up. Perhaps thinking it was a mirage because of the late hour — the ridiculous thought filtered through his addled brain.

"Wait, you don't need to leave yet. Come, sit. I can share what I've done tonight and tell you the good news! I've managed to get an appointment with a publisher after the holiday."

Following the tug of her hand like a damned puppy on a string, he took the seat opposite her as she dove into an explanation of the latest plot development in between holding up sketches of the creatures she'd drawn for the story and relaying her conversation with a publisher's secretary. They sat for long minutes, but Jonathan barely noticed the time passing, so captivated by her. Passion filled Hazel's blue eyes matching her fervid tone, though she made sure to keep her voice low to avoid waking the Kilneys. Apparently, Mrs. Kilney complained about thin walls when patrons occupied the establishment.

He admired her ambition and was amazed by her talent, but worry gnawed at him at the thought of future rejections. Because no matter how skilled of an artist or writer, she was still a young, single woman. With no name or impressive lineage to back her up. And he dreaded the day when that light of joy left to be replaced by defeat. If he could help her avoid such a fate, he would, but he wasn't sure what he could do when he had worse connections and blood than her.

"What do you think?" Hazel asked as she put down the final sketch of a porcupine with white-tipped quills.

"Hmm?"

"About adding another scene with Mr. Quill? Weren't you listening?"

Always.

But he couldn't tell her about his doubts, so instead, he took the opportunity to divert the conversation. "Of course, but it's hard to pay attention when we're alone in a room with your only protection, thin scraps of night clothing."

A sharp intake of breath and a hard swallow were her only reaction to the suggestive words. But then she licked her lips, and his gaze dropped to the motion, remembering their interlude last week and the pleasure that had followed.

Don't forget the ensuing argument, too.

He knew it was wrong. Isn't that what he told her? He knew they shouldn't continue down this path. But if the woman was as willing as she said, who was he to stop her?

"And what is it you think we should be doing if not talking about my book?" she asked.

Numerous visions bombarded him until one stood out, and he knew what he wanted more than anything. Pushing the leather club chair back, he crooked a finger. "Stand in front of me."

A breath passed before she stepped around the table to stand before him, his eyes level with her chest.

"Now, what?" The trepid whisper spoke of nerves yet held a note of curiosity. As an answer, he shifted to his feet, closing the space between them. Pushing the books and loose papers back to clear a space, careful not to ruin any of her work, Jonathan moved the table lamp to the floor before cupping her round bottom and lifting until she sat on the edge of the table. Her fingers dug into his shoulders in a quick grab for balance.

"Now, I want you to brace yourself like this." He positioned her bare feet on the leatherbound arms of the chair he'd been occupying. The move spread her legs and caused the white cotton dress to hike up her thighs, revealing smooth pale flesh to his heated gaze and the yellow glow emanating from the lamp.

"This feels very wicked."

A rumble of laughter coursed through his chest at the accurate assessment. Very wicked indeed, and he hadn't even started in earnest.

"I promise you'll enjoy it." Notching his cock to her center, he leaned in to take her mouth in a searing kiss. One of her hands lay trapped beneath his at her side, but the other reached up to grasp his neck, the short nails scratching. Invigorated, he deepened the kiss, the taste of chamomile from an earlier sip of tea urging him on instead of having its purported calming effect.

He loved that she gave as good as she got. No wilting miss, his Miss Taylor. While hesitant at first, she transformed after the first moments of a kiss as if actively freeing herself from society's strictures and choosing to enjoy the pleasures life had to offer. Pleasures *he* had to offer.

Tearing his mouth away, he ordered, "Lay down on your back."

"Why? I know I've allowed certain liberties, but I'm not ready to —"

"It's nothing like that. I won't take your maidenhead tonight. I've something else in mind."

She remained unconvinced, skepticism plain in her gaze and wrinkled brow, but eventually, she complied, slowly leaning back until her back rested on the mass of books behind her while her long hair draped over the other end of the table.

He wasn't sure how comfortable she was, but he intended to make any temporary discomfort worth it.

Reaching back to drag the chair closer, he took a seat and wrapped his arms beneath her legs, letting rough palms drift over the tops of her thighs as he struggled to drag a full breath into his lungs with his prize so close within reach. The blonde curls protecting her sex drew him like nothing he'd ever experienced before in his life. And he'd experienced a whole damn lot.

"What are you going to do?" Her anxious tone broke his reverie; it was time for him to stop tarrying. He didn't want her acceptance and nerves to morph into worry and fear. That's not what tonight was about.

"It's all right, sunshine. I'm just going to kiss you."

Taking a firmer grip on her splayed thighs, he brought her to his mouth like Galahad finally drinking from the Holy Grail. His thumbs spread her curls, allowing himself one long lick to savor her salty-sweet flavor before delving deeper in earnest.

"Jonathan..." Her back arched as a breathy moan rose from her lips. He loved the way she said his name, knowing it was the only one she'd ever cried out in her pleasure. "Yes...don't stop..."

A kernel of amusement nudged through the desire coating him. He should've known that even in this she'd be vocal. His woman liked to express herself — by writing, drawing, or giving instructions during lovemaking. But as much as Jonathan wished he could let her voice her passion, he knew it wasn't wise. They could be caught at any moment.

Reluctantly, he sat up, distracted for a moment by her prone form: legs wide, nightgown rucked up around her hips, hard nipples poking at the thin fabric. She was a map he dearly wanted to explore at length. Too bad he'd have to limit their play.

"Why'd you stop?" Hazel's disappointed tone brought another rush of mirth mixed with something akin to tenderness, but that wasn't something he wanted to examine at the moment.

"Don't worry; I'll satisfy you. But you seem to be having trouble keeping quiet which is imperative if we're to continue." Devising a plan, Jonathan grasped one end of her robe's sash and pulled it out from under her before walking to the other end of the table.

Hazel followed his steps, her knuckles white where they gripped the edges of the wooden table. He stood above her looking down at her upside-down face and couldn't resist dropping a kiss on her mouth — one that he found difficult to break.

"God, you're addictive," he whispered before raising his head and leaving behind a smear of wetness.

Fuck, that's pretty...

And you're depraved.

The sight of her own cream wetting her plump lips made his cock twitch, but he ignored it. This wasn't about him. Bringing the silken sash up for her to see, he dropped it lightly over her mouth, tacitly asking permission, waiting for her nod before tying it off.

"Now, where were we?" He returned to his seat and the dessert before him, slowly pushing two fingers into her hot channel until he could stroke the ridged spot at the top of her sex as his lips circled her pearl. A sharp gasp then a muted groan came from Hazel — the gag doing its job.

Something thudded to the ground, one of the books no doubt, when Jonathan felt the tell-tale quickening in her breathing as her sheathe clamped down on his fingers, and he sucked harder. Her orgasm sparked a stab of possession inside him as he kept pumping his fingers inside her, gentling his tongue until the waves subsided, and he built them up again. He wanted to be the only man to know her this way, however impossible the dream.

But Hazel's optimistic outlook on life stained him as well, encouraging him to believe in fairytales, apparently. Because with her sweet taste sliding over his tongue, with those adorable sighs of contentment tickling his ears, he could envision a future full of love and family with Hazel and Pete. She made him feel like he was a better man than his past would have him believe.

Time had no meaning as he continued pleasuring her until Hazel became too sensitive for his ministrations and began pushing at his head. Lifting up, he dragged her body towards his until she straddled his waist, lying limply in his arms. They were both sweaty and their combined harsh breathing filled the library. Carefully, he untied the sash and swiped it across his mouth and cheeks before dropping it to the floor and rubbing the edges of Hazel's mouth where red marked the skin.

"How are you feeling?" he asked, concerned that he might've pushed her too hard. She was a virgin, after all, no matter how far they stretched the boundaries.

"Exhausted." She covered a tired yawn before turning to nuzzle into his cheek. "But happy."

A brief kiss met his cheek before skimming closer to his mouth until their lips met, her body arching to press her breasts hard against his chest. But he couldn't let things escalate again, however tempting he found her charms.

"It's time for you to run along upstairs; it's late," he said, guiding her shoulders back.

"Not yet," she said, trying to lean closer.

"Yes, because your cunny squeezed my tongue and now my cock wants the same treatment." He spoke the crude words hoping they'd help her understand. "I already said I wouldn't take you tonight, and I'm not going to break my vow."

She hesitated as if seriously contemplating throwing caution to the wind, but he would never let her first time be anywhere but a bed where he had hours to spend discovering the wonders of her body. Firming his tone, he hefted her to her feet. "Now Hazel, before I lay you back on this table and fuck you hard, and there's no way the Kilneys won't hear you screaming my name."

The reminder of Hazel's landlords and boss galvanized her. Scampering away from him, she straightened her clothes, finding the soiled robe sash and tightening it around her waist. He watched as she organized the table, tucking her supplies under one arm. Once set to rights, she cupped his face and kissed him one more time. "Good night, Jonathan."

Then like the fairy in her story, she flitted away upstairs while he stayed a little longer trying to gather himself.

What the hell am I doing?

CHAPTER FOURTEEN

T he next morning Hazel found it difficult to leave her bed as the first rays of light peeked through the bedroom curtains. Only a few short hours before, Jonathan had surprised her with his visit and subsequent lovemaking. She imagined she still felt the scrape of his beard against her inner thigh and the insistent swipe of his tongue over her sensitive nerves.

Moistening dry lips, Hazel closed her eyes and allowed herself to drift back to that dreamy state. Shame or judgment remained at the periphery despite the knowledge that if anyone ever found out what she'd done — had been doing for weeks now — with Jonathan that she'd become a social pariah. At least, in her small circle. The Kilneys would terminate her position and kick her back to Hampshire where her sisters would wear disapproving yet concerned looks.

Not that Lily has any right to judge after that debacle years ago.

But she and Jonathan were careful, save for last night. And the idea of ending their relationship, however tenuous that description may be, created knots in her stomach and a pang near her heart. No, she would continue on for however long he wanted her.

Which may not be long at all...

Who knew when he'd tire of her? She doubted he ever wanted for female companionship. And those women probably reciprocated his advances. Sweeping a hand over her forehead in admonishment, she realized she hadn't done anything for Jonathan, only focused on her own selfish pleasure. Annoyance dampened her previous mood as she threw the blankets back and got out of bed.

It's not like he made it easy for you.

He'd simply taken control, and she'd let him.

Thoughts of what she could've done differently swirled in her mind as she performed her morning ablutions, donning a lavender dress, and joining the Kilneys for breakfast per her usual routine.

Walking into the austere dining room, Mr. Kilney perused the newspaper at the head of the table while Mrs. Kilney spread a pat of butter on wheat toast.

"Good morning," she said cheerfully. Filling a plate with bits of fruit and a poached egg, she sat across from Mrs. Kilney.

"Good morning, Miss Taylor." Mr. Kilney set his paper down to study her. "I went to the library earlier to look things over before we open, and I found *Mr. Gruff's Creatures* face-down on the floor. Pages are now bent and creased. Have you anything to say about this?"

Her eyes widened as scarlet heated her cheeks. "I apologize, sir. I must've accidentally knocked it off the table I was working at last night and forgot to pick it up. You know how engrossed I can become in my work." Which was true. Often people startled her when they tried addressing her while fixated on a task. Though she'd been occupied by something far more interesting than books last evening.

"That's no excuse for ruining inventory. This is my livelihood and patrons expect quality material. I can't have you destroying property during your personal time."

She hardly thought her actions warranted such an extreme reaction, but she did feel a measure of guilt for the evidence of last night's escapade.

"It won't happen again, sir. I promise."

"See that it doesn't," he said. "I took a risk hiring you with no references as a favor to your poor, departed father. But I'm afraid my kindness won't extend to more mistakes."

"And you've already accommodated Miss Taylor's charity work in Devil's Haven by extending her leave time," Mrs. Kilney added, causing her husband to nod in agreement.

"Yes, sir. I understand and thank you for your generosity." Her head bowed in deference as he picked the paper back up signaling the end of the warning. His comment about letting her go didn't sit well. What would she do? Go back to Hampshire? A failure in her family's eyes?

The rest of the morning passed full of mindless work as familiar numbness took over, obscuring any concern over the future.

Around noon, the bell above the library door tolled and Hazel looked up to find the man plaguing her thoughts in the flesh. Glancing around the room to see patrons perusing the shelves and ignoring the newcomer, she stood a bit taller as Jonathan approached the front counter.

"What are you doing here?" She blurted out the question in lieu of a greeting.

"Hello, to you, too." He chuckled, running a hand through already-tousled blonde waves. "I'm searching for another book on architecture. What would you suggest?"

"Architecture?" she asked dumbly. Her head tilted in confusion. What did architecture have to do with anything? Rational thought had clearly escaped her at his unexpected presence.

"You see, I'm renovating a building as part of a new business venture, and I thought it'd be a good idea to learn about the foundational —"

"Is this gentleman bothering you, Miss Taylor?" Mr. Kilney walked up, startling her out of her bewilderment.

"No, of course not. He's asking about a particular book."

Mr. Kilney eyed Jonathan up and down, taking in the worn pants starting to fray at the bottom and the jacket missing a button in the middle causing her to make a mental note to bring her sewing kit the next time she visited Devil's Haven.

"I don't think we carry anything you're looking for." The snobbish tone brooked no argument, and shock coursed through Hazel, quickly followed by anger at the insult.

"On the contrary, you have exactly what I'm looking for," Jonathan said, his gaze meeting hers before returning to challenge Mr. Kilney. The insinuation sent a flutter of butterflies flying around in her belly, but she hoped Mr. Kilney wouldn't suspect anything untoward between them.

And why should he?

For all he knew, Jonathan was only a visiting patron, one from a less affluent part of town according to his dress, but a patron, nonetheless. There was nothing to connect them. It was her own fear impairing her judgment.

"I'm afraid not, besides I don't recall you having a subscription to use the library. Now, if you'd be so kind as to leave; this is a respectable establishment. We don't need your kind loitering about."

Jonathan's fists balled up at his sides as pink tipped his ears, but he kept his voice low and even. "And what would that be, sir? *My kind*?"

Mr. Kilney huffed, lifting his patrician nose higher in the air. "If you don't know, then you're even more base-born than I thought."

A gasp fell from Hazel as she rushed around the counter to stand between the two men before their argument escalated to a physical altercation. Mr. Kilney was a slight man. He wouldn't stand a chance against Jonathan's sturdy strength.

"Gentlemen, please calm yourselves. You're causing a scene." Indeed, a few old biddies peeped over an opened book, pretending to read as they spied on the exchange.

Remembering his place, the library owner smoothed the front of his lapel before pasting on a fake smile. "Leave now or I'll hail for a constable." With that last threat, he turned to redirect the nosy women's attention.

"I think it'd be best if you do as he says," Hazel said, facing Jonathan whose frustrated gaze followed Mr. Kilney across the room. "If you're genuinely interested in architecture, I can bring something on my next visit."

"Don't bother. I wouldn't want you getting into trouble with that bastard."

"Shh...you shouldn't say things like that within his hearing. He's already on the verge of having you arrested just for being here. No need to add insults to the mix." She guided him towards the door, making sure to keep a professional distance between them, mulling over Mr. Kilney's reaction. She hadn't taken him for such a snob, though she knew he kept strict standards. Still, it wasn't like Kilney Library was the upper crust. It inhabited a decent part of town, but its patrons covered a wide range.

"I'm not worried about him. I came to check on you...after last night." A sweet look of concern passed over his face, engulfing her in a glow of security.

"I'm perfectly fine. You were extremely generous with your...attentions," she whispered.

"No regrets?"

She met his questioning green eyes and allowed a shy smile. "None."

Relief relaxed his shoulders as his face softened. "Good. Then, I'll see you tomorrow."

Nodding, she opened the door for him and leaned against the frame as she watched him lope down the stone steps and disappear down the street. A quiet sigh escaped her before she went back to sorting through returned books and avoiding any more trouble with Mr. Kilney.

"ANOTHER LETTER CAME for you, Miss Taylor," Mrs. Kilney used the side door into the library as Hazel finished closing up. The rotund woman waddled over with a small, folded parchment between her fingers. Thanking her, Hazel recognized the red seal and Caraway's neat handwriting. She stashed it in her pocket, for now, unwilling to open it in front of Mrs. Kilney.

After one last look around to determine everything was in its place and Mr. Kilney wouldn't reprimand her again, she bade the couple farewell and retired to her room. She asked a maid to send up a light dinner as she wanted to dine alone after the uncomfortable breakfast of the morning.

A quarter of an hour later, two slices of bread, two slabs of meat, and a bit of cheese became a hearty sandwich. The simple fare reminded her of home as she took a bite and examined her sister's letter.

Dear Hazel,

I hope you're well. It's been far too long since we've seen you, and with the holiday coming, it's the perfect time for a visit. I've arranged for a train ticket from Manchester to Hampshire for Thursday the twenty-fourth at nine am; it's all been cleared by Mr. Kilney. You'll return by the first of the new year.

Your frustrated sister,

Cara

Hazel stared in disbelief at the dictate. The twenty-fourth was tomorrow! And Caraway had secretly contacted Mr. Kilney to arrange the holiday? White-hot fury burned through her at the manipulation. Crumpling the paper, she tossed it on the table and shoved away the uneaten supper, no longer hungry.

She'd been lax when it came to responding to the multitude of correspondence Caraway, Iris, and Lily had sent her, but she'd been living her life — the whole reason she'd left Hampshire in the first place. Between work at the library, volunteering with the children, writing her book, and seeing Jonathan, no wonder things had fallen through the cracks.

Pacing the floor, she pulled the pins from her chignon to help relieve the building tension at her temples. Long curling waves fell to her waist as she shook it out, plopping the handful of pins in a ceramic bowl she kept for such a purpose and running her fingers through the thick strands.

Minutes passed before the bite of anger rushed to be replaced by guilt and a little bit of anticipation. Her sisters were only trying to be helpful; they wanted to check on the baby of the family. And honestly, she'd enjoy updating them on how much she'd thrived here. It would allay their initial worries, hopefully.

Yes, this was a good thing. Time away from work and more time to complete her book. The irony of returning home to write when that was part of the reason she left didn't escape Hazel, but she ignored the twinge of guilt in favor of positivity. It didn't matter how far behind she was in writing even if she'd expected to be finished by now. The end goal was the same and would still occur — her timeline only needed to shift.

One thing — person — kept her from feeling total happiness at the news of going home. Jonathan. She wouldn't see him tomorrow as planned then for a month more. Grabbing a piece of parchment and her pen, she sat down at the dining table, took a bite of her sandwich, famished again, and let Jonathan know about her changed plans. He would have to notify the children, too, so they wouldn't be waiting for her every afternoon.

Task completed, the rest of the night flew by as she tidied up and packed the small valise she'd brought.

Yes, this was a good thing.

CHAPTER FIFTEEN

Hand on the front gate, Hazel stood before her childhood home unsure of the feelings rushing through her. Nothing had changed in the months she'd been gone. Her walk from the village where the train had let her off had been filled with familiar sights: the small village shops, the fields belonging to their neighbor, the Earl of Trent, and of course, that bridge — long since repaired after the incident.

A bitter wind cut through her hesitancy to go in, echoing the bitterness she tried to keep at bay. Straightening her spine, a crisp breath cut through her lungs before she released it in a gust of heat and opened the gate to greet her sisters. They hadn't met her at the train station, which was fine by her. She was capable of walking the short way home, after all.

Her arm ached to drop the one traveling bag she'd brought, but otherwise, the exercise had helped dispel some of her nerves. With a knock on the door, Hazel let herself into the warmth of the cozy cottage — a blaze lit in the fireplace, and the smell of baked goods filled the space. Caraway, who sat reading by the fire, jumped up at her arrival as Iris who'd been working on her embroidery set it aside to follow at a more sedate pace.

"Hazel! You're finally here!" Her eldest sister pulled her into a tight hug then pushed her an arm's length away as she looked her up and down. "Well, you don't look the worse for wear after being in the city for so long. Come, take a seat and tell us about your trip."

"We're so glad you've come home for the holiday. We were worried you'd decide to stay in Manchester," Iris said softly. The frailest of the four girls, Hazel's cousin-turned-sister, exuded an ethereal aura reminiscent of an angel with her silvery blonde hair and grey-blue eyes. To be honest, she served as part of the inspiration for the fairy protagonist in Hazel's story.

"I'd never miss Christmas with my family; you should know that," she chided, squeezing Iris's arm. Setting her bag to the side of the door and removing her gloves and coat, she followed them to the kitchen area where Caraway began brewing a pot of tea while Iris and Hazel took seats across from each other.

"It's not so far-fetched to believe you might try to abandon us again," Caraway said with a pointed look. "You've already done it once with your abrupt move to Manchester. You very well could have become so attached to the city and your life there that you forgot all about your poor sisters. Your lack of communication certainly supports that theory."

Scarlet flushed her cheeks in guilt. It shouldn't surprise her that her minimal letters had been noticed. But what could she say?

Dear Sisters,

How happy I am to be out of Hampshire! Despite Manchester's gloom, I've found respite by reading to the children of Devil's Haven, one of the most dangerous rookeries in the city. Oh, and I'm having a scandalous affair with one of its gang members as well.

Best of love,
Hazel

Somehow, she didn't think that would go over too well — especially the part about Jonathan. Though to be fair, theirs was hardly a proper affair as it consisted of mostly kisses. *And when he found me in the library not two days past...*

More heat surged through her body than could be accounted for by the fire, and mortification seeped through her at such scandalous thoughts in front of her family.

"I apologize for my silence, but the library and my writing have kept me busy. The good news is I think I'll be able to finish my book while I'm here," Hazel said. Brushing a wisp of hair out of her eyes, she watched Iris and Caraway exchange a speaking look.

"How exciting...What are your plans for after it's finished?" Iris asked as Caraway joined them with the teapot, cups, and a plate of biscuits on a tray.

Reaching for the sustenance, sudden hunger gnawing at her stomach, she said wryly, "I've heard the next step is usually publishing."

"Yes, we know that, but have you found someone who will publish such a book from an unknown woman from Hampshire?" Ever the practical sister, Caraway's eyes narrowed in concern while her mouth became pinched at the corners.

"Not yet, but I have a follow-up appointment with a promising company called Steiner and Sons. They seemed amenable to my ideas." That wasn't entirely true, since she'd only spoken with the secretary who'd scheduled their future meeting. But she had high hopes. And if it could provide some peace of mind for her sisters, then what was the harm?

"That's good to hear, dear, but what happens if they reject your work?"

Her foot started tapping under the table as she took a sip of the hot tea. "Why must you immediately jump to that conclusion? Isn't it enough that they're willing to meet with me at all?"

Caraway sighed and reached across the table to place a hand on Hazel's arm. "I'm only thinking of your well-being and making sure you're considering all the possibilities. I don't want you to be disappointed —"

Having heard enough of this line of questioning, Hazel jerked her arm away and stood up. "Why can't you, for a moment, celebrate the *possibility* that I might accomplish my goal? That someone might actually like my work, see value in it?"

She crossed her arms over her chest, fingers digging into the cotton fabric, fearing she might fall apart. All of her life her family had indulged her creative notions, encouraged her imaginative musings, but now they acted as if she should ignore that part of her to follow a more stable path.

"I'm not saying what you're doing isn't valuable. We all had a healthy love of literature instilled in us by mama and papa, but you're not Jane Austen or one of the Bronte sisters."

"If only I were, then I'd have a sister who understood why I'm so passionate about writing and sharing my stories, who would support me instead of criticizing," Hazel said sharply as a well of tears began to rise in hurt and anger — the mention of their parents too much. This was why she needed to finish *A Fairy's Treasure*. To prove that she wasn't the flighty, young sister with her head in the clouds, dependent on her elder sisters to rescue her from certain failure. To prove it hadn't been a mistake for her to survive that accident when her parents' survival would've meant brilliant discoveries in their horticultural research.

Iris tried to bring things back to a calmer level. "We love you, Hazel. Perhaps we're going about it the wrong way, but we only have your best interests at heart."

Silence met her words. Hazel didn't know what else she could say to convince them to trust that she knew what she was doing. That she could and *would* make this happen.

Breaking the tense mood, the front door whipped open as Lily appeared in breeches and coat, her preferred attire for running through the forest, a favorite exercise of hers. She shrugged off her coat while taking in the varying degrees of upset on their faces.

"What's wrong now?" she asked, prepared to wade into their family squabble.

But Hazel refused to discuss things further, and the familiar numbness began spreading at her resignation, pushing away the frazzled emotions that had been batting at her like waves on the cliffs at Christchurch Bay. "Nothing. It's good to see you, Lily, but I fear the trip's left me weary. I need to lie down for a bit; excuse me."

"Hazel..." Caraway started, but Iris shook her head, and she stopped. Whatever she was going to say remained unspoken for the time being. Gratified, Hazel picked up her bag again and walked upstairs to the room she shared with Lily. With her mind blanketed in gauze, she unpacked the meager assortment of items she'd brought before changing into a nightgown, despite the early hour, and crawling under the wool covers.

She willed sleep to take her further into the blissful abyss of dreaming and away from meddling, doubting sisters.

CHAPTER SIXTEEN

Several days later, Lily and Hazel walked around the lake as a frosty breeze blew off the water. It was the first moment the two had managed to steal to talk just the two of them. Though Hazel loved all her sisters equally, Lily remained her closest confidante — even with her recent attitude.

"How are you faring? I heard Owen's returned," Hazel said. She knew Owen, their neighbor better known as the Earl of Trent now that his father passed, and Lily had a complicated past. They were once childhood sweethearts until something happened to tear them apart. Hazel never found out exactly what had occurred between her sister and their handsome neighbor — only that six years ago Lily stormed home in a fit, tears rolling down her cheeks. That Sunday at church scandal broke as one of the village boys called her a trollop after throwing herself at him. Owen disappeared to university before setting out on a tour of the Continent — somewhere he'd stayed until now.

The Taylor family weathered the maelstrom of judgement as they were already used to curious stares due to their unusual scholarly pursuits. The sisters had tried to get Lily to explain what had happened, but she'd clammed up tighter than a nun in a brothel, refusing to acknowledge their questions.

"And why should I care that he's back? We haven't spoken in ages." Lily tugged her shawl closer to ward off the chill and quickened her pace. The tallest of the girls, her long legs ate up the space, forcing Hazel to lengthen her own stride to keep up.

"Exactly. Did you two ever resolve your issues? And you never told me the full story of that summer. Perhaps I could help in some way," Hazel offered, though she was hardly versed in the ways of love. Her brief liaison with Jonathan didn't count. That wasn't love; it was exploring, enjoying his company.

A sharp "Ha!" fell from Lily's lips as she shook her head in denial. "There's nothing you could've done to prevent what happened and nothing you can do now to fix it. It's water under the bridge. Why, Owen Lennox, never even crosses my mind," Lily said.

Hazel didn't believe the lie for a minute. One didn't forget their first love even if he has been gallivanting around Europe. And now that he's back home? No, indeed, Hazel would bet her favorite pen that Lily thought of Owen quite often, and that he was in part responsible for her latest irritable mood.

They continued walking, lost in their own thoughts until a figure emerged from the copse of trees at the east end of the lake. The familiar shock of auburn hair caught her eye first before she recognized the loping stride of the man in question. Darting a look towards Lily, she saw that her sister had yet to notice the interloper.

What fun this will be...

"If you want to turn around, I'll cover for you," Hazel said quietly. Lily looked over; confusion clear on her face.

"Why would I..."

"Well, if it isn't the Garden Girls or two of them anyway." Owen's baritone voice rang out like a shot marking the start of a horse race — sudden and jolting. He stopped a few paces from them and bowed to their short curtsies. It always felt strange following propriety when they'd known each other since childhood and played together like siblings. But in the end, he was an earl's son, of the peerage, and they were the daughters of a scholar — not a drop of blue blood between them.

"My lord," Hazel greeted him, the words rolling around like gravel in her mouth. A noise sounding suspiciously like derision echoed from Lily, but she covered her mouth in the pretense of a cough.

"Miss Taylor," Owen drawled. "Surely, we can drop the formalities. I'm Owen, and you're Hazel — the little imp I chased through these very woods during hide and seek. I know time has passed since we last saw each other, but I will forever view you as the little sister I never had the pleasure of having."

His grey eyes drifted over to Lily, but he didn't speak, frustration and what looked like yearning appearing before being replaced by a neutral posture. "Miss Taylor." Interestingly, no *Lily* or *younger sister* comments for her, Hazel mused.

But Lily ignored his greeting, instead turning to Hazel. "I believe I've had enough of this wintry weather, dear. I think it's time to go back and see what Cara and Iris have cooked up for supper."

Hazel glanced between Lily's conscious avoidance and Owen's hard stare, uncertain how to defuse the tense situation.

It was unbearably rude to completely dismiss him, despite their past.

"Yes, I agree, Hazel. You must get out of this weather before catching a chill. Allow me to walk you home."

"No!" Lily drew back, placing a calming hand over her chest. "I mean to say, that's not necessary. We're perfectly capable of retracing a path we've walked a thousand times already. Good day, sir."

Clamping a hand around Hazel's arm, she dragged them both until they were out of sight of the lake and lingered by a large oak tree. Stark branches filtered the faint sunlight.

Lily discarded her arm as if it was afire and propped a fist on the tree trunk before dropping her forehead to the rough bark, a sigh escaping her — wilting much like her namesake in a drought.

"Do you want to talk about it?" Hazel asked, hating to see her sister in such turmoil, despite her earlier unbothered facade.

"Not at the moment. I'd like to be alone right now. Can you head home without me? I'll be along shortly." A sad tone seeped into Lily's voice, her shoulders drooping in defeat. Hazel wanted to wrap her up in a loving hug, but she knew it wouldn't be welcome. Not yet anyway.

"All right. I'll see you in a few minutes," Hazel said and turned to leave but wavered. "I love you, Lily. No matter what's gone on between you and Owen; you've still got me."

A watery chuckle brought a slight smile to her face. "Thanks, Haze. You don't have to worry about me."

But Hazel couldn't help it. Ever since their parents' deaths, the fear of losing her sisters had increased, something she'd never truly worried about before the accident. And while she may not lose Lily physically anytime soon, her sister had been drifting away, becoming her own little island for some time now. It pained Hazel to see someone she cared about so distraught, but she didn't know how to change things. Perhaps Caraway would know what to do. As the eldest, she'd always taken it upon herself to right her younger siblings' wrongs. Maybe she could figure out how to make things between Lily and Owen right again, but more importantly, how to return Lily to the former flame of herself.

Mulling over her options, Hazel traipsed through the crackling leaves covering the forest floor and breathed in the crisp air, allowing it to clear her mind, and providing relief from her own troubles.

Seeing a plume of smoke rise from the small cottage at the end of the trail, contentment bloomed within her. Soon it would be Christmas and, however disarrayed their lives may be, they'd be together as a family as they hadn't in months, celebrating the holiday with gifts and a smorgasbord of food. Not to mention celebrating Caraway's birthday as well. Good things were happening, and Hazel refused to let them be overshadowed by personal problems. December would come and go quickly enough. She didn't need to hasten it with worries about Lily or her writing or what would become of her and Jonathan.

Jonathan. She'd only been gone from Manchester for a week, yet she missed him. His kind support. His protective nature. And the passionate kisses.

Heat rose to her skin, melting any excess chill, at the thought of those intimate touches. Yes, she missed those, too, and she wondered if he felt the same way. If maybe he was thinking of her like she was thinking of him, and a ray of hope sprouted in her heart.

CHAPTER SEVENTEEN

The rookery lay quiet as Jonathan and Max headed back to Lucien's den to drop off the collected debts they'd gathered. A light grey showed on the eastern sky heralding the coming dawn which meant he'd be alone to obsess over Hazel soon. She'd left six days, ten hours, and twenty-two minutes ago, give or take a minute, and it chafed him that he'd kept track.

What did it matter if she'd gone home for the holiday? That he wouldn't see her until January which was three bloody weeks away.

It shouldn't bother him, shouldn't cause this restless feeling to rise in his blood every second he had time to think — when he couldn't shove it away to mindlessly do his work each night. Instead, like a specter, she haunted him, pervading his dreams with images of blonde curls and silken curves laid out on his bed, waiting for him to explore.

"You doing all right?" Max's gruff voice broke him out of the spiral he was falling into. *Christ.* Was he becoming so obvious that Max noticed something was off?

They crossed the cobbled street to enter a narrow alley that barely allowed Max to fit through with his giant of a body. "I'm fine. Ready to get some sleep. It's been a long night."

"They all are," Max said. Fifteen minutes later, after detailing the events of the night, they stood in front of Lucien as he smoked a cheroot.

"I see you're still here," he drawled. "Haven't left the nest yet, have you?"

Jonathan grit his teeth at the question. "Don't worry, it'll happen soon enough. Until then, I keep my word and prefer a job well done even if I'm resigning."

"Admirable." Lucien tapped the end of the cheroot on a tray before taking another drag. "But I don't think you will leave. The way I see it your word has been all talk about this boarding house venture, yet your actions tell a different story — working for me every night. It's got me thinking perhaps this is a ploy. You've sunk a lot of money into that ramshackle building, must be hurting for cash. You need more funds, boy, just ask. No need for theatrics and threats."

The convoluted reasoning boggled Jonathan's mind, and Lucien's facade of a benevolent manager took the cake. As if his position compared to a banker's or mill worker's where an increase of wages could be measured properly. And while the renovations drained his finances, he'd invested over the years in companies that helped him stay afloat. It never quite reached enough in his mind, but with Hazel's faith, he started to wonder if that wasn't his own insecurity instead of a true issue of funds.

"This isn't a ploy or trick. I just prefer to have all my chicks in a row, so to speak. When the house is ready for tenants, you will receive notice of my last day." Turning to leave, he caught Max's eye before walking out without another word — Lucien sputtering behind him at the dismissal.

He might pay for the rude departure, but the time for games was over. Lucien could choose to believe Jonathan or not; it wouldn't stop him from doing what he had to do. Stalking down the street, he wandered aimlessly around Devil's Haven.

His skin itched as if something ran beneath it — body vibrating with unspent energy. He considered heading to a tavern for a drink. *Or a woman*. Perhaps someone else would help rid him of his need for Hazel compounded by this latest fallout with Lucien, but he knew that's not what he really wanted. So, instead, he walked home, looking for a project, and found one.

An hour later he heard a sleepy voice call out.

"What's wrong with you?" Pete asked from the open doorway, rubbing the sleep from his eyes. It was still early in the morning, and Jonathan should be preparing to go to bed himself after the night's work. Yet he found himself in the makeshift schoolroom working on the menagerie of chairs and sanding their rough edges.

As if it matters while she's gone.

Selfishly, he wished she'd stayed in Manchester — with him.

"These chairs needed fixing, so I thought I'd handle it while it was on my mind."

"You wanted to sand broken chairs at this time of night? Didn't you just get back from Lucien's?"

Keeping his head ducked, fixated on a particularly stubborn knot, Jonathan grunted. "It was a slow night. Besides, if I have to hear Mary complain one more time about splinters,

I'm liable to toss the damn chair out the window rather than repair it. And what good would that do?"

"Miss Taylor certainly wouldn't like that...Is that what this is about?"

Jonathan's hand shook on the next downstroke causing the sander to skid off the side. "Why would you think that?"

"You've been acting strangely ever since you met her, and it's only increased since she's been gone," Pete said. "You like her, don't you?"

For a ten year old, sometimes Pete surprised him with his insight. Though growing up in the rookery caused children to mature before their years all the time, despite Jonathan trying to protect his brother.

"It doesn't matter. Nothing can come of it."

Running a hand over the smooth wooden surface and satisfied with the job, he moved on to the next leg. It'd take him a while to finish sanding everything before staining them.

"Why not? Miss Taylor's nice, and she seems to like you."

"It's not that easy, lad. She's a lady, and I'm no gentleman."

Understatement of the century.

A gentleman wouldn't sneak into a lady's place of work then proceed to fuck her with his tongue. No, he didn't think that was in the popular etiquette books.

"Miss Taylor doesn't care about social standing. She's different."

Jonathan couldn't argue his point, but she wasn't *that* different. Hazel still deserved a man of means, someone who could care for her properly. Instead of a man who only had a rundown building in the slums to offer.

Finished with this line of conversation, he set the sander down and walked over to Pete. "Come on, off to bed with you. You've got a few hours yet before school."

Once Pete was tucked in, Jonathan tried to calm the restlessness coursing through his blood with a hot bath, but the water didn't stop his mind from wandering to Hazel. And he began to wonder if there'd ever be anything to stop his thoughts from drifting towards her.

WITH A LAST FLOURISH, Hazel sat back, satisfied with the ending of *A Fairy's Treasure*. It had taken months, but she'd finally finished. Hazel closed her eyes, imagining a future where she walked into a publishing house, they loved her work, and they distributed it throughout the country, perhaps even the world!

Logically, she knew it wouldn't be that easy, but a girl could dream. And she had a well-exercised talent for dreaming. Moonlight filtered through the window casting shadows over the dim places her small candle couldn't reach, and the night lay quiet as nature slept. She wished she could run upstairs to wake her sisters to share the momentous news, but she didn't think they'd appreciate the action.

If only she were in Manchester.

Perhaps Jonathan would've snuck in again, and she could regale him with this minor triumph. In fact, she thought about writing to him, but fear held her back. Although they were friends — well, decidedly more, most days — they weren't betrothed or even courting. He may find a letter from her a bit too domestic or a signal of deeper feelings.

And while privately she could admit to a tendré for him, she never wanted to make him feel as if she expected him to reciprocate the sentiment. No, she'd wait to tell him about the book when she returned. This last week would be spent celebrating with her family and preparing for her next move once she was back in the city.

Jonathan could wait.

THE COTTAGE SMELLED of lye as the sisters finished cleaning from top to bottom before Hazel left, leaving them short a pair of hands. Standing in front of the frosted window in the kitchen, she stood folding their dried laundry and daydreaming about seeing Jonathan again. A secret smile of anticipation peeked out of the corners of her mouth at the thought.

"Hazel, hurry up with those. There's another basket waiting for you." Caraway squeezed her arm, startling her out of the dream, and her sister laughed. "Good to see some things haven't changed. You're as jumpy as ever when your mind's wandered off to the land of make-believe."

"I've actually missed spooking you," Lily added as she stacked clean dishes. "It's always so amusing seeing how high you jump."

"It's not funny. You've almost sent me into apoplexy at least a half dozen times."

"Worth it." Lily weakened the insult with a wink and continued her chores. It was nice seeing her in a good mood for once as they were so rare these days according to Caraway and

Iris. Owen's presence clearly weighed on her, but she resisted dealing with whatever issue lay between them.

"Don't tease, Lily. We wouldn't want anything to happen to Hazel." Iris piped up from her station polishing the silverware.

"Of course not..." Lily made a face that sent the girls into giggles, and a shroud of sadness coated some of her happiness. Despite their differences and the arguments they've had during this break, she loved her sisters and would miss them when she left for Manchester. Dot and Jonathan and Pete — they all provided some form of support, but no one loved and knew her like Caraway, Iris, and Lily.

Their bond ebbed and flowed like a river but remained mighty no matter their flaws and disagreements. Sometimes she forgot that.

"Should we make Hazel's favorite dinner before she leaves?" Caraway asked, bringing her back to the conversation. And she heartily agreed with the suggestion.

Dinner tonight with her sisters, then seeing Jonathan again the day after next.

It couldn't come soon enough.

CHAPTER EIGHTEEN

Cool night air swept over Hazel's face as she disembarked from the hired hack she'd taken from the train station to the Kilney Library. With bag in hand, she thanked the driver before heading inside. It'd been a long, bumpy trip, and she was ready for a good scrub and sleeping in her own bed. Being home had been the refresher she'd needed, but she wouldn't miss sharing a bedroom with her sisters.

Greyston opened the door for her arrival with a bow, and Mrs. Kilney greeted her as she ambled into the foyer. "Miss Taylor, I'm glad to see you've returned safely from your journey. How was your holiday?"

"Lovely, thank you. I can't express how indebted I am that Mr. Kilney allowed me the time with my sisters."

"Why, of course. He's a very generous man. Shall we expect you for dinner tonight?" The woman patted her coiffure and eyed Hazel's dusty traveling dress.

"I think I will retire early instead," she said, weariness settling on her shoulders. Mrs. Kilney nodded, and the two women carried on with their prospective paths — required pleasantries completed.

Although the hour was still early, Hazel knew it wouldn't take long for her to fall asleep. The wooden steps creaked with every footfall until she reached the door to her room.

A chill had settled in the month of her absence although a maid had kept the dust away. Sighing, she opened the door to her washroom and lit the small gas tank attached to the side of the tub to heat up her bathwater.

Undressing quickly, she laid her dirty dress across the back of a chair and stepped into the warm bath, sighing in immediate relief. The heat helped soothe her sore muscles from sitting all day. A tray stood by the tub holding a sponge and bar of soap along with a vial of lavender scent. Hazel poured drops of lavender into the tub, swishing her hand around to disperse it as the sweet smell bloomed in the hot water.

It didn't take long for her to lather up a handful of suds as she scrubbed the sponge over the thin layer of sweat and dust that covered her skin. She debated washing her hair but decided against it. The effort to wash and dry her long curls was too much for tonight when all she wanted to do was crawl into bed and sleep until morning.

Standing carefully, Hazel pulled the drain, climbed out, and dried off before tugging on a clean nightgown. *Finally*. Tying her hair quickly into two braids to keep it from tangling in her sleep, she finished her nightly ablutions and lifted one corner of the blanket to slip underneath when a small package revealed itself.

"What in the world?" Picking up the rectangle wrapped in brown paper, she examined it before pulling off the twine tied in a bow and tearing away the wrapping. A new set of watercolors appeared, and a wave of delight pushed back some of her fatigue. Would the Kilneys have left this for her?

Opening the smooth wooden case, a cream card with scrawled writing caught her eye. She turned to the candle yet to be blown out and read the bold words in black.

For your next book. J.

Sparks of light melted her from the inside out at the kind gift from Jonathan. She'd mentioned how her paints were running low in passing as she neared the end of *A Fairy's Treasure*. And now he'd taken care of the problem while expressing his belief that she'd write another book, too. Hugging the case close to her chest, she climbed into bed with a wide grin. This had to mean something. A man didn't leave a Christmas gift on a woman's bed for no reason, risking serious consequences if caught in her bedchamber.

Closing her eyes, sleep whisked her away to a world of dreams filled with Jonathan and a bright future together.

HAZEL JOLTED AWAKE. An uneasy feeling washed over her as she opened her eyes to glance around the room. It was late. Moonlight streamed across the wooden floorboards, casting looming shadows. Her heartbeat pounded in her ears as she held her breath, trying to figure out what had caused her to awaken.

A shuffle from the corner caught her eye, and she watched as a man emerged.

"Jonathan?" Relief tore through her along with a rush of energy as all her fear converted into...something else that set off sparks in her blood.

"I didn't mean to wake you."

"How'd you know I was back in Manchester?"

"I've had someone watching the library. I knew you were bound to return sometime this week," he said with no guilt or shame over having someone stalk her home. His reasoning confused her, though.

"But why?"

He tugged at his coat sleeve, avoiding her gaze. "I'm not sure I can explain it myself...How was the visit with your sisters?"

She let him change the subject, though curiosity ate at her. First, he had someone watching for her return to obviously notify him immediately. Then he takes to breaking into her room instead of waiting for her to come to the rookery.

"Despite the auspicious beginnings with Caraway's summons, it felt nice being home for the holiday. My sisters still worry about me, but I think they're coming around to the fact that I can take care of myself."

"They're right to worry," he said, moving to sit on the edge of the mattress, eliciting a creak from the slats holding the bed up.

Shifting her pillow, so she could sit up, Hazel crossed her arms over her chest. "I think I've done well so far. I have a job, volunteer in Devil's Haven, and I've finished my book." She dropped that last bit of information to see his reaction. She'd been itching to tell him for days now, and here he was finally.

A proud smile lit up his face. "You finished it? Congratulations! I knew you could do it."

Blushing, Hazel ducked her head at the praise. "Thank you. It's a relief to finally say it's completed. I was starting to sound like a broken record saying I was writing a book but not having anything to show for it." Insecurity reared its ugly head, but she pushed it away. She'd done it. She'd seen it through to the end.

"I never doubted you. Now, you've only to find a publisher."

"Ah, yes, the easy part," she said with a laugh.

"I have faith in you."

"As I do in you," she said. "How is the renovation going? And your holiday? You must be close to being able to start having tenants move in."

"Not quite that close."

"Nonsense. I've walked through the building, seen what you've done. It's ready, I tell you."

Shaking his head at her vehement belief, he held a hand up. "Let's table the conversation for another time. I don't want to argue with you."

"What *do* you want to do with me?" The brazen question popped out before she could stop it.

"You shouldn't ask that question, sunshine. It's dangerous."

"I'd say we're already erring on the side of danger with you in my bed at this hour."

"I'm not in it; I'm on it. There's a difference. A thin but important one," he countered, though he edged closer.

Hazel leaned forward until their lips touched in a searing kiss that spoke of their longing for each other after so much time apart. His beard scraped against her cheek, and she welcomed the physical sensation as his tongue swept inside her mouth. Strong and insistent, the kiss morphed from sweet yearning to carnal need as Jonathan pushed until she was laying back against her pillow with his body covering hers. Frantic hands tore at clothes and the wild movements caused an ominous creaking to shatter the moment.

"This isn't going to work," Jonathan said before sweeping her up and down to the floor. Hard floorboards met her back as Jonathan's hand crept up her legs, lifting her nightgown with it. "We shouldn't be doing this, but I can't stop. If you want me to, you're going to have to end it."

A pleading note entered his voice, and Hazel wondered if it was a plea for her to tell him to stop or for her to let him continue. "Don't stop. I want this, too."

"Thank God." He crushed her mouth under his and cool air wafted over her bare skin as he revealed her thighs, then higher as he tugged the thin piece of cotton over her head. Lying naked beneath him, she knew she should feel self-conscious, nervous, but all that really coursed through her blood was excitement and anticipation. Everything they've done so far had been leading to this. And now they'd each have the ultimate satisfaction of their needs.

Carnal eyes skimmed from her face to her breasts to her core as a groan of lust fell from Jonathan. A shaky hand traced down the center of her chest until he cupped one breast in his rough palm, his thumb stroking the budding tip. "You're perfect."

A self-deprecating laugh bubbled up. "Hardly."

He glanced up at her denial. "It's true. I've never held such perfection in my arms, yet here I am ready to defile you. You should tell me to leave."

"You're not defiling me. I'm giving myself to you because I want you. You're the only man I want," she said, her tone brooking no argument.

"How is that possible?" he asked the question but didn't seem to need an answer as he dropped his head to kiss along her collarbone. Her hands tangled in his hair, holding onto the thick strands for security. His mouth trailed lower until he flicked her nipple with a teasing lick before sucking softly. Their heavy breathing filled her ears as all of her senses converged on that one point. Nudging his head, she urged him to her other breast where he gladly accepted the invitation and repeated the attention. Long minutes passed as he alternated back and forth until her nipples stood swollen and red.

A shudder ran through Jonathan as he stared transfixed at his handiwork until he shifted lower. This was familiar territory, and Hazel couldn't deny a tremor of eagerness.

"Open for me, love." Jonathan's request was immediately answered as she let her legs fall open, forced wider as he fit his large body between her thighs. "So wet and pretty for me. Aren't you?"

She didn't respond. Couldn't as his tongue circled her opening before thrusting inside. Her walls tried to hold him there, but he retreated and licked up through her folds to find the center of her pleasure. He turned to rub his cheek against her like a cat and the bristles of his beard itched, uncomfortable, a harsh contrast to his tongue but somehow heightening her desire.

"Please...Jonathan..."

"Shhh, have you forgotten already? I'll take care of you. Don't I always?" His words penetrated the haze of lust surrounding her and made her wonder if it meant he felt more for her than a passing fancy. He'd admitted to wanting her, yes, but never for a determinate amount of time. But this almost sounded close to commitment.

You can't think about that now. Not when the man's head's between your thighs.

He tongued her sex before sucking the engorged nubbin, alternating between soft and hard pressure. She felt his fingers dip inside her and rub against a particularly sensitive spot. The combination ratcheted up her desire, and it wasn't long before it sent her crashing into an orgasm. But she didn't have long to enjoy it before she felt him pull back and watched as he removed his clothing. Large swathes of skin enticed her to explore as she followed the hair on his chest down a firm stomach to his hardened member. Licking her lips, she imagined kissing him as he'd done to her.

"Not tonight, love. We'll get to that soon enough." As if he read her mind, he winked and returned to her. The heat from his exposed skin melted into hers, and they both moaned at the contact. Rubbing her hands up his arms to his shoulders, she adored the play of muscles showcasing his restraint as he held himself above her.

"Hazel."

His questioning tone made her look up — a softness had entered his gaze. "This may seem like a foregone conclusion at this point, but we can still stop. I haven't breached your maidenhead yet."

It touched her that he was willing to check once again on the state of her emotions. That he cared if she was still with him.

"I don't want to stop." She cupped his cheek and smiled. "You, Jonathan Travers, are the only man I want to give myself to. I'm yours." And she meant it even if he'd never agree to keep her.

Nodding, he adjusted himself at her center and slowly pushed inside. A stretching, burning began, and she tried to breathe through the pain. It wasn't entirely horrid, and it was expected. All she'd heard about when it came to the opposite sex was the pain that came with consummation.

"Hold on." Jonathan paused in his entry, surprising her, as he reached down and began circling her clitoris. He continued stroking until she forgot about her pain and lifted her hips to urge him onward, needing their union to be completed. Inch by inch, he sank into her, pausing as needed when she'd tense up, always continuing his stroking of her nubbin, until finally he could go no further, fully seated within her channel.

"Are you okay?" he asked, the words coming ragged from his labored chest.

"I'm fine. It wasn't as bad as I thought it'd be once you started...um..." She blushed, embarrassed to say the words aloud even if she was a grown woman lying here with her lover.

"Your pearl, nubbin, clitoris." Jonathan listed the synonyms with a grin, making her laugh then groan as the movement shifted him inside her.

"Right. That." She agreed then bit her lip. "Is this all there is then?"

"Ready for it to be over, eh? No, love, I was just waiting for you to relax some more, which I'm guessing has happened."

She nodded in assent and gasped as he pulled out, his cock dragging along her walls before plunging back inside. Over and over, he repeated the action, starting slow and picking up speed. The floor beneath her had no give; she couldn't escape his pounding thrusts. But she didn't want to.

Something was building in her blood. Something stronger than she'd experienced before. Worried about making too much noise, she forced Jonathan's head to hers for a kiss as her body released the pent-up tension, her body bowing, and her cry of pleasure muffled by Jonathan's mouth. It didn't take long for him to follow her into oblivion, a couple jerky thrusts until he pulled out — a sticky warmth landing on her stomach.

"Why'd you do that?" she asked after a breathless moment of recovery, curiosity breaking through her fatigue.

"To protect against getting you with child. We're already risking enough without adding a babe." The words came out winded as he levered himself above her. She appreciated the forethought, though, a tiny illogical piece of her wished for that tie.

Don't be ridiculous! An unmarried pregnancy couldn't come at a worse time.

Jonathan rolled to the side but kept an anchoring arm around her waist. "I don't want you leaving again. Promise me."

The quiet plea shook her, tossing her from one impossible wish to another. What did this mean? Could he have serious intentions towards her?

"You can come with me next time," she said. If someone would've told her hours ago, when she'd arrived back from Hampshire, that she'd invite Jonathan home with her someday, she would've laughed. Yet here she was doing that very thing, and the idea had merit. No matter their differences, her family would accept him. They weren't ones for ceremony, already seen as eccentric considering their upbringing.

He groaned and sat up, running agitated hands through his disheveled hair. "I can't go home with you. Your family won't want you associating with a criminal."

She noticed he didn't mention anything about a lack of emotions for her. Hope blossomed in her heart. Perhaps he felt what she did. "My family isn't like that. They'll accept you...love you..." As far as declarations go, she wasn't sure what she was doing, but she wanted to see his reaction to the possibility of her love.

"Hazel..." He turned and stroked one of her braids, coming undone after their previous activity. Moving to kneel in front of him, the hard floor beneath digging into her knees, she braced herself with hands on his shoulders and ran comforting kisses over his face.

"Trust me. The Garden Girls of Hampshire are not your normal, run-of-the-mill English misses. We grew up with a scholar for a father and our mother was just as educationally inclined. Most days they let us run wild over the countryside, so they could focus on their studies of the different plants in our gardens. We don't discriminate against people for their background when we've been looked at oddly all of our lives." She finished her explanation with a decisive nod of her head.

Not to mention the debacle with Lily.

"While that sounds democratic of you, I doubt it'll be the reality once they meet me." He sighed. "Forget I said anything. It wasn't my place to ask for promises from you anyway."

"I don't mind. I didn't like our separation either. As much as I enjoyed spending time with my sisters. I missed Manchester and the children." *And you.* But she'd revealed enough of her heart tonight. Best to keep some things secret lest her heart be trampled on completely.

"You did?" His emerald gaze tried to decipher the veracity of her words.

"Yes, this is my home now. I don't belong in Hampshire anymore."

"You think you're a city girl now?" he joked.

"Well, I'm not far off, now, am I? I make my own living working at the library, maintain my own finances, and I manage to volunteer. I even finished writing a book in my spare time."

"Very industrial of you."

"Quite. As industrial as the city of Manchester." They both smiled at the teasing banter as she sat beside him and bumped his shoulder with hers before leaning her head on him, covering a yawn as fatigue caught up to her.

"I should let you sleep. You've had a long day," Jonathan said. He stood before reaching to help her up, too.

"No, don't go. Stay for a little while longer."

"I don't think that's a good idea. We're already risking a lot by my being here."

"We won't be caught, I promise." He still looked skeptical. "Please. For me." She took a hold of his hand, clasping it tightly and tugging him back towards the bed.

Relenting, he followed her, quickly grabbing her discarded nightgown to clean his spend from her body before they were both tucked under the blankets, the creaking bed slats stopping once they'd settled with him curled behind her, his heat creating a cozy cocoon that hastened her sleep.

"Goodnight, Jonathan." Hazel held the arm around her waist close, bringing his hand up to her heart and closing her eyes, content in his arms.

"Goodnight, love. Sweet dreams." She felt him brush a kiss over her earlobe before burying his face in her neck. They both fell asleep together as if it'd occurred many nights before, the routine of an old married couple comfortable in their ways. And Hazel prayed that one day that dream could come true.

CHAPTER NINETEEN

H azel stretched her arms over her head before cuddling into the blankets. Soreness permeated her muscles and a slight ache throbbed from her core, serving as a reminder of the hours before with Jonathan. He'd taken her once more as twilight broke through the curtains — a slow, sweet possession compared to their earlier lovemaking.

I'm no longer a virgin.

Guilt should be flooding her, but she had none. The past months spent with him had been building to this, and she couldn't deny the pleasure he'd given her. Last night had been a revelation. Growing up in the country and as a daughter to scholars, she'd known the mechanics of sexual intercourse, but that knowledge had proved useless in the face of Jonathan's tender care.

The things he'd done...

Renewed heat surged beneath her skin. Best not to think of that for the moment.

Sunlight washed the room in a dreamy glow she wished she could bask in for the entire day, but today would be her first day back in the library. She couldn't call off after such a generous break provided by Mr. Kilney. Allowing herself a few more minutes, Hazel drifted in a hazy state of contentment before shaking it off and starting the day.

Heading downstairs to open the library, Mr. Kilney stood at the front counter. Odd. Usually, he arrived after her, but maybe he'd forgotten she'd be back today.

"Good morning, Mr. Kilney. How was your holiday?" she asked as she faced him, smoothing her hands over the glossy wooden top, polished to perfection.

"Miss Taylor, I need to have a word with you." His stern tone surprised her. Apprehension knotted in her stomach as she followed him back to his office and took a seat in front of his desk. It remained clear of clutter, only a lamp, two neatly stacked books, and a pen lay on top.

"Is something the matter? Did something happen while I was gone?" She rested clasped hands in her lap and tried not to jump to any worrisome conclusions.

"I like to walk in the morning; it helps me start the day clear-headed."

Her brows furrowed at the strange sequitur, unsure of how his exercising habits would be of any concern to her.

"Usually I'm up before daybreak, and I can watch the sky lighten from pink to orange. That is if the weather decides to cooperate. By now, I'm sure you've realized Manchester days are far greyer than you're used to in Hampshire."

"Yes, sir, I've noticed..." The unusual line of conversation heightened her anxiety causing the knot of worry to tighten.

"Today dawned without a cloud in sight — very rare. The street beamed with light, and as I finished my walk I watched as that ruffian from before snuck out the back door like a thief, which I presume he is. I can only infer that he came to see you upon your return."

Her eyes widened in shock. "Mr. Kilney, I can explain —"

"I don't think you can, Miss Taylor. You're an unmarried young woman consorting with a man who is not your husband. I had a feeling something sordid was between the two of you after the familiar way you greeted him."

Sordid? No. What they'd done went against societal norms, but it wasn't sordid. That made it sound dirty.

"My wife and I run a respectable business, and we don't abide by such wanton behavior. What would your father think if he knew what you'd been doing?"

That pierced her shock and all the non-existent guilt from earlier came crashing to the forefront. Her father and mother would be disappointed, especially after the incident with Lily. Yet, she'd allowed her personal desires to overcome rational sense and jeopardized her position.

"I'm afraid you're dismissed. You'll need to pack your things and leave by the end of the day," Mr. Kilney said with finality. Standing up, he went to the door and opened it, gesturing for her to leave.

"But sir, you must understand. I didn't mean to...That is to say, I never..." She struggled to vocalize a reasonable explanation for what he'd seen, but none could be found. It was exactly as Mr. Kilney thought: Jonathan had spent the night in her bed, and that wasn't acceptable behavior from respectable women.

He shook his head in refusal. "There's nothing you can say to change my mind. You must be out by the time the library closes or else I'll have to call a constable to escort you out."

The threat hung heavy in the air, nearly choking her with fear. Galvanized, she raced past him, tears welling in her eyes as she blinked rapidly and took the stairs two at a time. Locking the door, she sat on the bed before laying back and staring at the ceiling. Slow tears tracked down her cheeks, and she blinked at the burning sensation.

What was she going to do? She'd just returned from Hampshire only to turn around and go home? What would her sisters say? How could she explain why Mr. Kilney would terminate her position?

She dragged a ragged breath into her lungs — tearing at the neckline choking her throat — and closed her eyes as visions of the disappointed looks on her sisters' faces flashed before her. She couldn't tell them the truth, of course. They wouldn't throw her out, but they wouldn't understand what had compelled her to give away her one asset in the eyes of good society.

Lily might understand.

When the questions converged and it all became too much, a calming wave of numbness settled over her like an old blanket causing her worry and fear to drain away as the struggle to breathe retreated.

What's done is done, the apathetic thought resounded in her mind. *It's your own fault you're in this mess. You've mucked up your future — proving everyone who doubted you right.*

Listlessly, her gaze glided around the room. It wouldn't take long to gather her belongings as she hadn't gotten very far unpacking the night before, and none of the furniture belonged to her. Hours lay ahead before she'd need to leave. But where to go?

Jonathan.

His name brought a bit of warmth that managed to seep through the protective numb layer. Could she bother him with her troubles? *You've given him your maidenhead, the least he could do is help you figure out what to do next.*

But he didn't owe her anything. She gave herself to him with no expectations. Could she really turn around and call on him for help? *Yes.*

Yes, she could. Even if as only a friend.

Jonathan wasn't a monster. No matter a romantic attachment, she knew he'd care enough to want to offer aid. It was in his nature. Subdued with the thin plan, she wiped a hand over her wet cheeks, erasing the evidence of her sadness, and stared about the sparse room. Her home for less than a year, it'd still been her own. Hers alone not to share with sisters or anyone else. A private sanctuary she'd never had before, and now she'd been cast out, forced to find a new refuge.

All will be well. You'll see.

Go find Jonathan.

CHAPTER TWENTY

Jonathan sat at the kitchen table watching Pete tear through his breakfast of toast and jam while he contemplated the night before. He hadn't been thinking clearly — going to Hazel. But when the man he had watching her home returned to tell him she'd come back, it'd sent a jolt of lightning through his body, expelling the restlessness he'd felt for the past month and ushering in a chaotic sort of energy.

He'd needed to see her. A compulsion like nothing he'd ever known had overcome any common sense he might've possessed, and he'd found himself in her bedroom before he even realized it — traipsing through the somber Manchester streets as if in a trance with one target in mind.

"Slow down before you choke," he warned as Pete stuffed another large bite into his mouth.

Huffing in annoyance, Pete exaggerated a slow bite before going back to breakneck speed. Jonathan didn't understand the rush; it wasn't as if the food was about to be snatched out from under him. But he supposed living years in the rookery had taught Pete to take what you have while you got it or else. Although Jonathan always made sure his brother was looked after.

A faint knock filtered back to them, and he wondered who it could be, praying it wasn't a lackey sent by Lucien for another random job. Sometimes he liked to conduct certain business in the light of day, and Jonathan handled it.

Forcing himself to answer the door, he took a fortifying breath before opening it to find Hazel on the doorstep, her small fist raised to knock again. Red rimmed her eyes as he took in the unusual paleness of her skin and the valise in her hand. Something was wrong.

"What's happened? Are you all right?" he ushered her inside, out of view of any nosy neighbors, before trying to take the bag from her — a feat as he uncurled the white knuckles curled around the cracked leather handle. Once it was finally in his grasp, he set it aside and pulled her stiff body into his. Straight as a board with limp arms at her sides, he hugged her tighter, hoping to elicit some sort of response.

"Hazel, sweetheart? What is it? You can tell me."

"What's wrong with her?" Pete's voice reminded him they had an audience, and he shifted so his back was to his brother, shielding Hazel in her vulnerable state.

"I'm not sure, lad. Why don't you fetch a cup of water for Miss Taylor then head off to school?" He heard light footsteps retreat behind him before returning a few minutes later.

"I set the cup on the side over here. Is she going to be all right?" Worry laced his little brother's tone, but Jonathan couldn't do much to comfort him at the moment as he was trying his best not to upset Hazel.

"She'll be fine. Run along now before you're late." Once Pete left with the slamming of the back door, Jonathan bent his knees and swept a hand under Hazel, hefting her into his arms and carrying her to his room upstairs. The bed remained unmade, blankets tossed wildly about, as he carefully maneuvered them onto the mattress.

Leaning against the headboard with Hazel cradled in his arms, he tried again to get a response — her practically catatonic state frightening him. A sense of deja vu hit him in the chest because she had reacted the same way after her attack.

"Hazel, I can't help you if you won't speak to me."

"Mr. Kilney saw you this morning," she said, sounding as if she were far away. "He saw you leave the library."

Dammit. He thought he'd been careful, left undetected, but clearly, he'd been wrong.

"What did he say?"

"He expressed that he wouldn't allow a fallen woman to work for him and how my father would be disappointed in my behavior. He gave me until the end of today to leave. I didn't know where else to go, so I came here." She turned her head into his neck, the words becoming muffled. But he understood all too well.

This was his fault. He'd jeopardized her job and home. *You did this, you selfish bastard*. For all his spouting off about becoming a changed man and leaving the old Jonathan behind, the proof of his failure glared in his face.

"You did the right thing. I'll fix this." But how?

Hazel echoed the same sentiment as he tried working out a plan. He doubted Mr. Kilney would accept any sort of explanation from him, and really there weren't any acceptable excuses.

"I know what I have to do. I'm just not ready to accept it yet."

"What do you mean?" Foreboding crawled up his spine at her resigned tone.

"My savings will only last me so far without a proper job, and I doubt I'll be able to secure a position so soon or at all without a reference from Mr. Kilney. He only hired me in the first place out of loyalty to my father." Her voice wavered as she toyed with a loose thread on his shirt. Only a few short hours ago, the same movement had occurred as she caressed the hair on his chest after another bout of lovemaking.

How the tables have turned from that moment of contentment.

"You're smart and capable. Anyone would be lucky to have you. We'll find another position."

"I don't think so." Hazel struggled to a sitting position; her skirts tangled between their legs. "I have to go home."

"No," he growled the word, panic rising in his chest. She couldn't leave.

"Jonathan."

"No, we'll figure this out. It's my fault this happened, and I'll handle the consequences. I can fix it." A sick desperation entered his tone as a cold sweat broke out on the back of his neck. Hazel couldn't leave. She'd promised him last night.

"No, you can't. There's no guarantee I will find another position, at least not before my savings run out. Maybe this will be a blessing. I'll go home, start contacting publishers and potential employers, and I won't have to worry about paying for boarding or meals."

"I'll take care of you."

"I know we've strained the bounds of propriety to the breaking point, but I draw the line at letting you pay for my living. I won't be your mistress."

"It won't be like that," he denied.

She ticked off points with her fingers, some of her previous energy returning. "You would be paying for my sleeping arrangements, my food to survive. And what have I provided in return? I let you into my bed. Sounds like a mistress to me."

Another solution floated around in his head, but Jonathan couldn't suggest it. Could he?

"Marry me."

"What did you say?"

"Marry me, and you won't have to worry about leaving." Jonathan warmed to the idea, the easy solution fighting off his prior despondency. "It makes the most sense. You already spend most of your time here teaching, and Pete could use feminine guidance aside from Mrs. Wilson. It's the perfect solution."

"You're serious? You want to marry me?" Hazel asked, wide eyes searching his.

"It's the only way for you to stay without reprimand. And while I know I'm no catch and Devil's Haven isn't Peel Park, the marriage will be legal, and no one can fault you then."

A silence fell between them as she contemplated his proposal. He knew it was extreme, but what other choice did they have? Refusing to examine his reasons too deeply, he didn't want her to leave, but she couldn't stay unattached with no support. A disastrous situation created by him, it was only right that he fix it by any means necessary.

Besides, it's the practical decision for Pete. Hazel would make sure he stayed on the straight and narrow, becoming an educated member of society away from the Cobblewallers — a victory for everyone. Yes, that's why she needed to stay — not because Jonathan couldn't do without her.

"Yes, I'll marry you," she said. Relief flooded his system, and he crushed her to him in a hard embrace. "But I'll still need to go home to tell my sisters and for the wedding. I can't imagine what their reactions will be, but they'll agree to my wishes."

Jaw tightening in discontent, Jonathan muttered, "I thought the point was to avoid returning to Hampshire."

"It'll only be for three weeks, enough time for the banns to be read and prepare a small ceremony. This may be sudden, but I want my family to be present at my nuptials. We can at least try for a semblance of propriety."

With the decision made, Jonathan didn't like the idea of being separated from her again so soon, despite her sound reasoning. They were already bucking the boundaries, best to try to keep one thing on the up and up. Especially when her family would soon become his in-laws. The wise move would be to keep them on his side — however difficult it may be considering he ruined their sister.

"All right. We'll marry in Hampshire. I'll get everything sorted for the marriage license and Lucien before joining you."

Nodding vigorously, Hazel's haphazard curls continued to spring from their pins. "Do you think I can catch a train today? I'm not sure I should spend the night here even if we are engaged."

"Then let's get you to the train station; it's still early. I'm sure there's another one scheduled for Hampshire."

They both climbed out of bed and returned to the front entry. What a change a half hour made. He'd started the day a bachelor; now he had a fiancé. But at least the color had returned to Hazel's cheeks. Jonathan never wanted to see her in such a pained state again.

"We're really doing this?" Hazel asked as he grabbed her bag.

"Yes, we are. No backing out."

She smiled brightly and clasped his hand briefly before heading outside. The dye had been cast — they would wed. Hazel would be his, and no matter how ill-prepared he was to be a husband, he was committed to caring for her and seeing to her happiness.

The underlying feelings of why it mattered so much to him hovered on the edges of his mind, but he rationalized them as lust and practicality.

She's best for Pete and you find her attractive in every way, leave it at that.

CHAPTER TWENTY-ONE

"I was wondering when you'd arrive," Caraway drawled as Hazel stepped inside the cottage with no warning knock. The admission stopped her in her tracks.

"How did you know I was coming?"

"Mr. Kilney sent a telegram apprising me of the situation. What were you thinking? Sneaking around with a man? Have you forgotten what happened to Lily?" Each question aimed true like an arrow to her conscience. Dragging in a strained breath, she walked to her favorite stuffed chair and sank into the comforting cushions — the day wore on her, and she wasn't done yet.

"Where's Iris and Lily? They'll want to hear this, too." It would be difficult enough going over the events leading to her dismissal the one time.

"They left for a walk an hour ago and should be back soon," Caraway said, sitting across from her. As if summoned, the two women in question strolled inside.

"Hazel! What are you doing here?" Iris hugged her tightly before stepping back. Hazel shot a glare at Caraway over Iris's shoulder. Clearly, she hadn't shared the news she'd received.

"Something's happened. You might want to take a seat for this." She gestured to the sitting area by the fire, waiting until everyone was situated before launching into the events of the past two days — purposely keeping the night hours between her and Jonathan vague, though a shared look of knowledge passed between the women as they read between the lines. Then she dropped the biggest revelation of the past twenty-four hours: her engagement.

"What?"

"You're engaged?"

"You can't be serious!"

Three separate exclamations battled for supremacy as Hazel clasped her sweaty palms together in an effort to calm frayed nerves.

"I know it's sudden, but it's necessary. My time with the Kilneys has run its course, and marriage to Jonathan will provide a way for me to continue pursuing writing while teaching the children."

"I still don't understand what you were thinking. How could you do something so drastic since the last time we saw you."

"You mean two days ago?" Lily snorted. "You know how flighty Hazel can be, following her heart before fully thinking things through. Case in point: her move to Manchester and now this."

"That's not fair," Hazel said. "I'd contemplated leaving for a while but didn't know where to go."

"But you didn't even mention this Mr. Travers. And now you're going to marry him?" Iris's light brows crinkled in confusion as she wrung a handkerchief between her hands.

"It's the best choice to allay any nasty rumors the Kilneys may spread and to allow me to continue my work in

Manchester. Besides, I truly care for him despite keeping his existence a secret from you all."

"We can weather whatever may come from gossip. We've done it before." Caraway glanced at Lily who'd shifted her gaze towards the fire heating the cottage.

"Perhaps, but why invite more scandal when a marriage can solve everything? This is what I want." She wouldn't be swayed. Smoothing her palms down the wool of her dress, she waited for the next volley from her sisters, yet silence saturated the room.

Caraway bit her bottom lip, the tell-tale sign of her running through all the possible solutions to their current dilemma, until a decision was made with a clap of her hands. "Right, well, it looks like we'll be hosting a wedding. I'll see if I can find Mama's dress, so we can tailor it to you, Hazel. Iris, would you mind visiting the Trent Estate to see if Owen would mind housing Mr. Travers as a guest? He can't stay here, the village inn seems a bit impersonal, and I'd like to get Owen's measure of the man."

Like a general barking orders, she took a breath before launching into another list of items to be done. Bemusement lightened Hazel's mood at the familiar scene. Responsible to a fault, her eldest sister could always be relied upon for setting a plan and directing them to execute it.

Releasing some of the tension in her shoulders, she sank into the chair and let her mind wander to Jonathan — wondering how he fared with his own list of tasks before he arrived in Hampshire.

A FORTNIGHT LATER, Jonathan and Pete stepped off the train platform and walked to where Hazel sat in an open carriage, waving excitedly. Another woman with matching curls sat next to her holding the reins to a chestnut horse.

"Jonathan, Peter! You've made it!"

"Miss Taylor!" Pete ran up to the carriage as Jonathan followed behind with their bags.

"Peter, we're going to be family; you must call me Hazel now," she said before turning to the woman on her right. "And this is my eldest sister, Caraway. Cara, this is Peter and Jonathan Travers." She gestured to both of them as he neared the group.

"It's a pleasure to meet you. Welcome to Hampshire."

He doubted she was truly pleased with their arrival since he was a complete stranger preparing to marry her sister, but she hid any reservations well as her expression remained pleasant.

"Thank you; we're looking forward to getting to know Hazel's family," he said as they climbed into the back of the carriage and the horse started ambling down the road.

"As we are you. We've taken the liberty of arranging accommodations for you with our neighbor since our cottage isn't large enough for guests, not to mention it wouldn't be proper to have the groom staying so close to the bride with the nuptials only days away." Hazel had written to notify him of the arrangements, mentioning staying with a neighbor of theirs. He supposed the fact that their family friend was willing to accommodate him and Pete along with Hazel's sister being civil was a good sign. Worry had gnawed at him the entire time he'd been in Manchester preparing for this visit, fabricating scenarios of angry sisters with pitchforks refusing him their sister's hand in marriage.

Ridiculous to be sure.

"You'll love staying at Trent House. Oh, and Owen!" She said the name with such fondness that jealousy curled in his stomach. He'd imagined an elderly neighbor from her letter, but the note of familiarity in her tone suggested something different.

"Yes, don't forget him. The Earl of Trent. Your host for the next week." Caraway elaborated as astonishment burst in his gut.

A fucking earl?

"And he's okay with strangers staying with him? I'm sure we can find something in the village. There must be an inn nearby." He studied the small shops they passed before the road opened to bare-branched trees and barren fields. The winter landscape a different tableau from what he was used to. Nearly thirty years and he'd never left the city boundaries.

For good reason, apparently. He couldn't believe Hazel had left out such an important detail as their neighbor being an earl.

"Nonsense. Owen is happy to have you both, and his mother, the Dowager Countess, is one of the kindest women you'll ever meet." Hazel looked back at them with a smile. "Don't worry; it's not a problem."

And he wondered again at the close bond between the man and Jonathan's soon-to-be wife.

They traveled with only the clopping of hooves on the dirt road breaking the silence, each occupant lost to their own thoughts. Eventually, they stopped in front of a little cottage surrounded by a white fence. Shriveled vines climbed the aging brick while shrubs and sleeping flower patches dotted the yard.

"I thought you could meet Iris and Lily before we continue the journey to Owen's," Caraway explained.

He and Pete hopped out of the carriage, and he went to help Hazel but both women had already jumped down. The front door opened to reveal a wraith of a woman with silvery blonde hair in a coronet around her head.

"Welcome to Rose Cottage. I'm Iris. How was your trip?"

"Exciting! We were going so fast everything blurred together. I've never seen anything like it," Pete exclaimed as his eyes sparked around the idyllic scene, ever the outgoing personality. Jonathan regretted not exposing Pete to more experiences like this earlier. For all his talk about Pete exploring the world beyond Manchester, he'd done little to actually help him do that.

"It's quite the ride. Come in, come in. It's cold out here." Iris waved her hand, motioning them inside. "It'll be tight but cozy."

"Nothing we haven't dealt with before." The tallest sister plopped down in a chair in front of the blazing fire heating the small space. That must be Lily. He eyed the breeches that conformed to her legs, surprised to see such a thing.

Hazel warned her family was peculiar...

Jonathan and Pete squeezed into a worn loveseat while the women scattered around the room in a jumble of chairs. "Hazel says that you're about to open your own boarding house? Seems like a lot of work for one man."

And so the inquisition begins.

"I'm hoping to hire our current housekeeper for a full-time position which will help, but I'm no stranger to hard work," he said firmly. From his time as a chimney sweep at five years of age until now, earning everything he owned was an ingrained habit.

"But you'd still expect Hazel to assist as the lady of the house? Would that leave time for her personal pursuits?" Caraway conducted the interrogation with the skill of a spymaster ferreting out information. "Which also brings up the question of living quarters. Do you plan on residing with your tenants in the boarding house?"

Originally, that had been his plan, but now he saw there would be a need to find a separate home for the three of them and any future children down the line. A growing family required space to thrive.

"Really, Cara, could you try to be a bit more accommodating? The man just arrived, and you're pelting him with these —"

He cut in. "It's all right. Your sister has every right to ask these questions. I expected no less." Met with varying degrees of welcome from each sister's gaze, he continued. "As soon as we're able, we'll find our own residence outside of Devil's Haven. And as far as Hazel's ambitions, she has my full support. I'd never ask her to compromise such an important part of herself."

The silver-haired waif sighed as a dreamy smile formed on her mouth, but the other two women weren't so easily swayed by pretty sentiments. Clearly, they would reserve judgement — actions speaking louder than words and all that. But Jonathan found it encouraging to have at least one Taylor in his corner besides Hazel.

More questions followed his declaration, but the toughest part was over. Soon they moved into discussions of the wedding before it was time to leave for the Trent Estate. Their group loaded into the wagon again while the two remaining sisters waved goodbye as they set off down the road. A short ten minute drive later, and they stopped before a large manor with stone steps leading to double doors.

It was hands down the most spectacular place he'd ever been to, and a tangle of unworthiness battered around in his belly.

Pete's mouth hung open as his eyes took in the palatial home. "We're staying here?"

Hazel and her sister laughed and patted him on the back. "It's quite a change from what you're used to, hmm? To be honest, I sometimes stand in awe as well, despite growing up seeing it almost every day," Hazel said.

Gathering their paltry belongings, the Travers followed the women to the front entry where the doors swung open upon their quick knock. Stepping inside, Jonathan saw a man younger than he expected standing in the foyer along with a butler and an older woman.

"Owen Lennox, Earl of Trent." The man offered his hand to Jonathan for a firm handshake. "Welcome to Trent House. My mother, the Dowager Countess, and I look forward to hosting you for your nuptials to our dear Hazel."

His endearment rankled. And once again Jonathan questioned the relationship between Hazel and this earl. First, she mentioned being around here a lot as a child, and now His

Lordship was letting her betrothed stay under the same roof. It spoke of an intimate relationship he didn't like.

"Thank you for opening your home to me and my brother," he said, forcing politeness. Large, framed portraits of a lineage going back hundreds of years surrounded them, reminding him that he could barely go back three generations before his blood was muddied.

"Yes, we appreciate your hospitality, Owen."

"Anything for Hampshire's Garden Girls," Trent said, a teasing glint in his grey eyes — the familiarity in his tone itched at Jonathan's skin. Possessiveness warred with common sense as he considered showing this earl exactly who Hazel belonged to.

"You know we don't care for that moniker," Caraway said from her stance by the entry, arms crossed over her chest.

"Yet it fits so well."

Caraway looked heavenward as if praying for deliverance and released a beleaguered sigh — clearly, this was a continuing battle. "If you're agreeable, I think it's time we take our leave and let the two of you get settled. We'll call on you tomorrow. Hazel?"

"I'll see you both soon." Hazel hugged Pete, shooting Jonathan an encouraging smile that soothed a measure of his ire. "And thank you again, Owen. We truly appreciate your generosity." With those parting words, the sisters left the three of them alone in the foyer with the staff.

Turning to the older woman, Owen asked, "Mrs. Kemp, would you please show Peter to his room? I'd like to speak with Mr. Travers for a moment."

Here it is. The moment Jonathan had been waiting for.

"Follow me." The earl started walking down the hall until they ended up in an office dominated by the oak desk sitting in front of large bay windows. Warm sunlight filled the room, and Jonathan prepared himself for some sort of stand-off.

Trent stopped in front of a window, staring out at the manicured lawn with his hands behind his back. "Jonathan Lee Travers. Twenty-nine years of age. Associate of Mr. Amos Lucien of the Cobblewallers Gang. Mother and father deceased. One ten year old brother, Peter Dean Travers." He paused and faced Jonathan after listing the broad strokes of his life thus far.

"So, you had me investigated. Can't say I'm surprised, though I wonder why an earl takes such an interest in a country family."

"I consider them my family as well, and it doesn't sit well that one of them is about to marry you," Trent said. "However, Hazel has made it clear that she won't retract her acceptance of your proposal, no matter how persuasive her sisters and I try to be."

He'd expected Hazel's sisters would have qualms about the youngest's impending nuptials, but it burned that this man presumed to sway her decision against him.

"I see...Hazel's free to do as she pleases. I'm not forcing her to marry me if that's what you're getting at."

"Oh, she's been quite insistent everything's being done of her own volition. But I warn you — if you harm her or, by extension, her sisters — I won't hesitate to use every resource in my power to see you two are separated, and you're sent far away," Trent threatened. Jonathan's teeth ground together, and his fists clenched tightly as he resisted pummeling the man for making such a suggestion. Hell would freeze over before he'd be sent packing without Hazel.

Arrogant prick.

"Threats may work to cow the people in your employ or polite society, but I am neither. I'm from the rookery, born and raised, taught to protect what belongs to me at any costs. And let me be clear: Hazel is *mine*." The last word stating his possession came out on a growl. He didn't care if this man was hosting him until the wedding; he'd sleep out under the stars if it came to it. He'd slept in worse conditions.

"Time will tell," Trent said cryptically. "Until then, I'll leave the conversation at that as we've both made our positions clear. I'll send someone in to show you to your rooms." Imperious edict handed down, the earl swept out of the room with all the nobility his blood gave him.

Jonathan's fists ached to knock the man down a few pegs, but it wouldn't do to assault his host. Inhaling a slow breath, he waited until his blood cooled to a more natural level and went to find Pete in their shared suite — guidance from a passing maid necessary as the earl's home resembled a labyrinth.

Stepping into one of the bedrooms, he found Pete jumping on the enormous bed, disrupting the dozens of pillows decorating the head of the mattress. "Having a bit of fun, lad?"

Pete dropped down to his back, spreading spindly arms and legs outward. "I've never seen something so big. Can you believe Hazel is friends with an earl?"

"It was quite a shock to me as well." He sat down by the boy and patted his leg. "I've been meaning to ask how you feel about Hazel and I marrying."

Sitting up to rest on his elbows, Pete smiled. "I think it's wonderful. Now she can stay with us all the time. She can become my teacher, and I won't have to see Miss Crenshaw anymore!" The boy's enthusiasm forced a short chuckle from Jonathan. Of course, his only concern was avoiding school with the strict educator.

"You know Hazel's passion lies with publishing her book. I'm not sure she'll have time to teach full-time. And don't you remember her reaction to being called that name?" He raised his eyebrows in question, recalling the afternoon when they argued over teacher versus tutor.

Pete's face screwed up into a frown. "I forgot about that..."

"Teaching aside," Jonathan pressed. "You don't mind her coming to live with us? She won't be your mother per se, but it'll be good to have a womanly presence around to keep us men in line since Mrs. Wilson isn't always around to finish the job."

Pete plopped back to the bed and stared up at the velvet draping hanging overhead. "Nah, I don't mind. Everyone's going to be jealous that she'll be my sister-in-law."

Appeased by his answer, Jonathan joined his brother and laid down beside him. "They're right to be jealous. Hazel's as rare as they come. It'll be our job to look after her."

"Don't worry, everyone knows not to mess with the Travers men." Pete's matter-of-fact tone charmed him. His brother really was a good boy. Despite the building collapse and death of their parents that led to their closeness, despite his own feelings of regret at his past selfishness, it was the one silver lining to come from that day.

CHAPTER TWENTY-TWO

The next day, the Taylors and Traverses along with Owen toured the village finishing last minute wedding preparations while introducing the newcomers. Hours flew by, and it wasn't until later in the afternoon that Jonathan and Hazel had a private moment to talk while Peter spent time with her sisters. With her arm tucked through Jonathan's, they traced the familiar path to the lake.

"Alone at last."

Hazel chuckled at the relieved note in his voice. The past two days couldn't have been easy for him with new faces and an environment so different from Manchester. Trees surrounded them as opposed to brick buildings standing in close quarters, and the difference was jarring.

"Soon we can be alone as much as we want, then you'll be saying that same line only locked away in a closet somewhere to avoid me," she joked.

"Never." He shook his head vehemently. "It'll probably be the other way around as often as I feel this need to be near you."

Leaves crunched beneath their boots — brittle, brown, and dead. Something she never wanted their relationship to become, and his admission was as close as he'd come to voicing any sort of significant feeling for her, alleviating some of her fear.

"Two peas in a pod, then. We'll never tire of each other." She knew that wouldn't hold true forever but knowing how difficult they found it to resist each other boded well for the future. *Unless the clandestine nature of our relationship thus far was the only motivator for such a strong pull.*

The path ended on a grassy patch surrounding the pond, and they continued to walk along the edge of the water passing an old marble gazebo tucked into the forest. As children, they used to pretend it was its own island since a small creek branched off from the main water source leading to a moat around the structure. The only way to access the island was by crossing three stones set in the water.

"I hope that's true..." Jonathan said, drawing her attention. "How do you think Pete's faring with your sisters?"

She appreciated the switch of subject as they moved to lighter conversational ground. "Oh, he loves the attention. I'm sure he's never had so many women doting upon him."

"You're right, though Mrs. Wilson does a fair job of making up for it."

"It's a shame she decided not to come down with you two, but I'm glad she'll be here for the ceremony." The woman had cited someone needing to hold down the fort at home while they were gone, but Hazel wondered if she feared being an inconvenience.

"I tried persuading her, but she wouldn't budge." He shrugged in resignation causing his jacket to strain across the shoulders. Resting her head briefly on his arm in commiseration, she sighed.

"I like how we tried turning to a more positive topic only to end up melancholy thinking of Mrs. Wilson," she said as they reached their original starting point and began the trek back to the cottage. It wouldn't do to be out much longer unchaperoned. Her sisters were probably already eyeing the clock, counting down the minutes before they returned.

"And I fear I'll have to heap more serious topics on the pile. Your sister brought up a good point about our living arrangements and my current job position."

Her brow wrinkled. "I like where we live, and it'll only be more interesting once we have tenants."

"We can't stay there forever. I don't want to raise my family in Devil's Haven, growing up there myself provided enough reason to exercise caution. It'll be safer for Pete outside the Cobblewallers grasp." She hadn't considered that notion, but the fact that Peter very well could follow in his brother's footsteps disturbed her.

"You're right, of course, about Peter. Speaking of the Cobblewallers, how did Lucien take your leave of absence for the wedding?" Barren branches cast shadows over his face as they slowed their walking the nearer they got to the cottage.

"He congratulated me." Surprise laced his tone. "Then mentioned something about how it wouldn't be prudent to leave him now that I'd be saddled with a wife. He seemed under the impression that you would beggar me with expenses if I didn't continue working for him."

"Hmm...I think we both know that's not true. However, I'm glad to hear you left him in a genial mood. Perhaps he won't be so resistant when you quit. Despite all of his blustering, he hasn't actually threatened violence against you, correct?" Worry for Jonathan's safety ate at her, though she knew he could take care of himself. Most of the time, she was able to forget the dangerous work he completed, since she never saw that side of him. But times like these reminded her that there was an entire underworld Jonathan inhabited that she knew nothing about.

Jonathan murmured something under his breath neither confirming nor denying her assessment. "Let's forget Lucien for the moment. We need to take advantage of our privacy before returning to your family. And I can think of one thing I've craved doing for weeks now." He stopped them in the middle of the path and wrapped his arms around her waist. Their heat mingled together to ward off the January chill. "A kiss for the affianced couple. I believe we skipped the tradition when I proposed."

Rueful grins blossomed at the memory. "We had more pressing matters to attend to if I recall — my fall into ruin and unemployment." With some distance from the fateful day, she found some amusement in how everything went wrong so quickly.

"You may have a point there. Good thing I'm a reasonable man and decided to take you in." He winked and tightened his embrace.

"Ah, yes, reasonable...Especially since you aided in my ruination. Had quite a starring role, I believe." He hummed in agreement before closing the gap between them and pressing his mouth to hers. Letting her lips fall open with a contented sigh, she slid her hands up his chest to circle his neck and hold him to her. She adored his kisses — the soft and sweet or frenzied with passion. Each one made her feel seen and wanted.

His tongue slid along hers in retreat before he placed a farewell brush of his lips against hers and pulled back. "That'll have to do for now. We should get going before your sisters send out a search party. I don't want to press my luck too far."

They quickened their pace back home where they found Peter standing on a stool while Caraway took measurements that Iris wrote down. "What's going on here?" she asked.

"We're double-checking the fit for Peter's wedding suit. How was your — What happened to you? You're all red." Caraway motioned to her cheeks.

Heat skittered down her body as she realized her sister was talking about the beard marks left by Jonathan who coughed into his fist as he came to the same conclusion. "It's cold outside. It's only natural to look flushed after such bitter winds."

"Bitter winds? It's not that chilly outside..." Laughter sparkled in Iris's eyes as Caraway clucked her tongue in disapproval but refrained from another comment. Shooting a pleading look towards Jonathan for any sort of diversion to rescue her, he launched into a discussion about Peter's outfit. Thankful for the reprieve, Hazel sat by Iris and welcomed the sight of her sisters and the Traverses chatting amiably.

This will work.

Her two worlds colliding but not crashing.

HOWEVER, IT WASN'T to be smooth sailing until the end with her sisters. On the eve of the wedding, they couldn't resist voicing their concern one more time.

"Are you sure you want to go through with this? There's still time to beg off."

"For the last time," Hazel said in annoyance, "this is what I want. I'm marrying Jonathan Travers tomorrow."

The four sisters sat on a blanket covering the floor, their nightgowns flowing around them as they enjoyed their last night together without husbands or future children. Iris lay with her head in Caraway's lap as the latter brushed her hair in soothing strokes.

"Of course you are," Lily said from her perch against the end of her bed, back resting against the mattress. "Instead of asking if you're going to marry, we should be discussing what happens afterwards."

Caraway laughed. "The horse already came before the cart in that respect."

The reminder that her sisters knew such a personal detail sent a blush to her cheeks. She feared they would never let her forget it either.

"I, for one, am curious how it was."

"Iris!" The girls giggled at her curiosity, but they all stared at Hazel waiting for her answer.

"I'd read enough of Papa's books on biology. I was well-prepared." A slight fabrication, but how could she explain the sensations, the emotions? Nothing but experience could truly capture the moment.

"Reading and doing are two very different things," Lily said, keeping her gaze averted, and once again, Hazel wondered exactly what had happened all those years ago.

"I wish Mama were here. She'd know what to say." Iris's voice floated on the air — ethereal and light like its owner. Guilt crept along Hazel's veins. If only she hadn't wanted to go to the neighboring village to see a visiting troupe. The accident never would've happened.

All her fault.

"Yes, but we mustn't wish for things we can't have. And thinking of Mama and Papa will only make us sad," Caraway said. "As for you, Hazel, are you ready for tomorrow?"

Fastening a smile on her face, Hazel nodded. "I'm sure. Jonathan can be quite kind, you'll see. But enough about me. It's all we've talked about for weeks. We should try to decide who will be next!"

"Not me," Lily said with an emphatic shake of her head. "I'm never getting married."

"Don't say that." Hazel placed a hand on her knee. "It'll happen."

She scoffed at the optimistic promise. "No one wants to marry the ruined Taylor girl, and I can't say I blame them." Shifting, Lily laid down and stared up at the ceiling, her arms resting above her head.

"You're not ruined." Lily whipped up to a raised position for a rebuttal, but Caraway hurried on before she could speak. "Your reputation is tarnished, but a worthy man won't listen to gossip. He'll love you for who you are — not some indiscretion of your youth."

"What an imagination you have. You sound like Hazel. And where can I find this paragon of a man because, surely, he's pure fantasy."

"He exists...He may even be closer than you think," Iris drawled, ever the romantic.

"I hope you're not insinuating what I think you are." An edge entered Lily's voice at the topic of Owen — the only man

Iris could be talking about. At times, it was difficult balancing their deep friendship with Owen and their sisterhood with Lily, but she'd told them to do as they pleased. Whatever occurred between her and their neighbor was a private matter that should have no bearing on their own relationships.

"It's been years. Maybe the both of you can —"

"No, we can't, and I don't want to talk about it anymore. This is Hazel's night. I may be sick of hearing about floral arrangements and the breakfast menu for tomorrow, but it's better than this line of conversation." A tension-filled silence fell over the room until Caraway's quiet voice spoke up.

"Tonight's the last night we'll all be together like this. Everything will change tomorrow." Her somber expression echoed everyone's sadness at the realization.

"Everything's been changing ever since Mama and Papa's deaths," Iris mused. "We lost them, and now we'll be short a Garden Girl."

"It's not as if I'm disappearing forever. I'll visit as often as I can, and you can come to Manchester whenever you want. Instead of losing me, consider how you're gaining two brothers."

"Because the surrogate one we have isn't enough." Everyone but Lily chuckled at Caraway's statement — the vision of Owen teasing and protecting them like a sibling coming to the forefront.

"Can you imagine if Jonathan and Owen banded together?" The idea sent a collective shudder through Hazel, Iris, and Caraway.

"If your husband tries to dictate to me like Owen, I won't be responsible for my actions." Lily pointed a finger at Hazel in warning, but she held her hands up in conciliation.

"I'll try to keep him in line." Yawning, the weight of the evening caught up to her. "I believe that's my cue to call it a night. The bride should look refreshed on her wedding day, after all." They helped each other to their feet and hugged — Caraway holding on a bit longer to Hazel than necessary before separating to their beds.

Crawling in next to Lily, Hazel sighed in contentment. Tomorrow she'd be a married woman.

Mrs. Jonathan Travers.

CHAPTER TWENTY-THREE

"Dearly beloved, we are gathered here today to witness the joining between this man and this woman." The curate droned on enumerating the many blessings of marriage before having Jonathan and Hazel say their vows. Sweat collected under his arms as his formal suit made him feel like an animal on display for the village guests attending the ceremony.

He wasn't used to such attention, and it was starting to wear on him.

Don't mess this up. Pay attention to Hazel.

A vision in cream lace and silk, she shone like the sun he often compared her to. Blonde curls held back with combs cascaded down her back, and he itched to touch them.

Soon.

Clasping hands, they exchanged rings, and finally the ceremony ended to celebratory applause. The wedding breakfast would be held at the Trent Estate, so their small procession made its way from the tiny country church amid hearty congratulations and slaps on the back.

Thankfully, everything flew by in a haze and before he knew it, he and Hazel arrived at the cozy hunter's cottage Trent had offered them for their wedding night before they left on the morrow.

Lavender and rosemary decorated the hunting lodge walls — the fresh scent of herbs enveloping them as they stood surveying the room. The layout was simple with the bed in one corner while a hearth provided separation from a tiny kitchen area. "Owen outdid himself or rather his servants did. This is beautiful."

"Is there something between the two of you?" Jonathan asked the burning question he'd held inside for the past week. It was unfortunate timing, and he hadn't meant to blurt it out, effectively breaking the mood, but he had to know.

Hazel whipped around; her eyes wide in surprise. "What? Me and Owen?"

"That would explain why an earl is willing to open his home to strangers. Offering this lodge for our wedding night. Why he pulled me aside to warn me about hurting you."

She shook her head. "That's just Owen. He's always been protective but like an older brother. His interest lies with Lily."

"Lily? They barely say two words to each other whenever they're in the same room." It had struck him as unusual since the rest of the Taylors fawned over Trent — the feeling mutual — except for Lily.

"They had a falling out years ago, but Lily and Owen were childhood sweethearts. I'm sure they'll work out their differences soon enough now that he's back." Hazel walked up to him and gently massaged his shoulders, rigid with tension. "Which means there is absolutely nothing between us, never has been and never will be. He's like a sibling, nothing more."

She searched his gaze as if trying to discern whether or not he believed her. Considering her explanation, he thought back to the interactions he'd witnessed between them and how, when he thought about it, Trent did seem to have a fascination with the tallest Taylor, his eyes always tracking her, even if they rebuffed each other.

Realizing his mistake, the effect of jealousy rearing its ugly head, a sigh of relief left him. "I believe you. It's just difficult for me to understand why a peer of the realm would be so welcoming."

"Know many peers, do you?"

He chuckled. "No, but one hears things."

"Well, they may be true for most noblemen, but Owen's different. Maybe it's because we all grew up together, but he's never let his title go to his head. You may have noticed we don't call him "My lord". It's because he's practically adopted us as the siblings he never had." She smoothed her hands down his arms to grasp his hands. "Now, if we're done talking about him, we have a wedding night to attend to."

And just like that, his priorities shifted. She was right. They were married which meant he had certain responsibilities.

"You have a point, Mrs. Travers." He liked the way the title sounded on his lips. *Mrs. Travers.* He had a *wife*. "Why don't we make you more comfortable?"

"And how do you propose to do that, Mr. Travers?" Cheekiness had entered Hazel's voice, and he looked forward to exploring this playful side of her.

Drawing a hand up her back, he circled to the top button of her dress. "I can think of a few things." Slowly, he loosened the closures one by one causing her dress to sag under the weight of the fabric. Bending forward, he nuzzled her neck, kissing up the fine column to her cheeks before meeting her lips in a sweet kiss that quickly turned frantic.

They tore at each other's clothing until skin met skin, and he guided her to the freshly-made bed. "Wait." Hazel turned to face him.

"Is something wrong?"

"No, I... Before we progress much further, I was hoping I could kiss you like you kissed me." Her eyes dropped to his erection, and her meaning became clear.

"You want to do that?" Hazel constantly surprised him, but this was different. He'd only ever had to pay for such a pleasure, and as eager as he was for her, it worried him that she'd hate it — realize such an act was beneath her.

"Very much. If I can...That is, if you want..." She motioned towards him before swiping a shaking hand over her forehead. He found the nervous gesture endearing and decided to let the chips fall where they may; he wouldn't stop her from trying.

"I do. Just tell me where you want me. I'm yours."

Truer words were never spoken.

Raising a hand, she pointed. "You stay there, and I'll..." Her gaze fell towards the head of the bed and grabbed a pillow before tossing it to the floor and kneeling before him. "This works, right?"

"Yes, but are you sure you wouldn't be more comfortable on the bed?"

"We'll get there soon enough, don't you worry." A teasing glint shone in her eyes as her small hands rested on his hips. Considering the sight of his raging cockstand, Hazel bit her lip in consternation. "There's quite a bit more of you than me to take in, hmm?"

"If you're having second thoughts..." He offered another reprieve, willing to wait until she was ready.

"I'm not, just making an observation that this type of lovemaking seems a bit easier on your end. Are you sure we'll fit?" One hand moved to wrap around his staff and raised it to her mouth where she gave a delicate lick.

Choking a little at the sensation, he nodded. "Positive. We were made for each other." The flowery sentiment sounded out of place coming from him, and honestly, it made him uncomfortable. A man from the rookery knew better than to spout poetic drivel, but Hazel didn't seem to have the same problem if her sudden smile was anything to go by.

"Made for each other," she repeated before feathering more kisses and licks over him. Burying his fingers in her hair, he prayed he could stay upright even as his knees weakened.

Christ, she's barely begun, and you're about to spoil her enjoyment by coming too quickly.

Directing his attention to the wall in front of him, he watched the flames dancing in the fireplace, a groan escaping when Hazel finally enveloped him with a shallow thrust of her mouth. Rubbing her tongue beneath the head, she repeated the bobbing motion slowly.

Oxygen serrated his lungs, breathing turning difficult. What was she doing to him? He'd never had this reaction even with practiced women. A hesitant hand reached beneath him and cupped his stones, gently stroking, and causing him to jerk in surprise. Cool air replaced wet heat as Hazel swiftly retreated. "Did I hurt you? I didn't mean —"

Swallowing hard, he shook his head. "No, you just surprised me. I didn't expect you to..." He licked dry lips, unsure of what to say, then decided blunt is best. "Carry on. I liked it."

She studied his expression for a moment before trusting his assertion and continuing her ministrations. The combination of her mouth and hands created a maelstrom of sensations in his body, and it wasn't long until the tell-tale sign of his impending peak made itself known.

"Hazel, love. You must —" But the warning cut off as his cock spasmed and shot his seed down her throat. *Fuck.* Like a green boy, he shuddered with the force of his orgasm, holding tight to Hazel as she rode the wave with him, swallowing enthusiastically until he finished and pulled out.

Unsteady on his feet, Jonathan stepped backwards and fell into a chair, propping boneless arms on his knees before dropping his head to take deep breaths. A soothing caress smoothed over his back while Hazel murmured soft, unintelligible words that somehow helped calm him.

"Good God, woman, what you do to me." He managed to spit out after another minute passed.

"I think that's meant to be a compliment?"

Looking up at her amused face, he dipped his head in agreement. The glow from the fire limned her body — plump curves with intriguing shadows — and he rallied for another round. But this time, they'd try something *he* wanted. Turning her to face the mattress, he instructed, "Your turn. Climb up on your hands and knees."

She shot him a quizzical look and tilted her head. "Why?"

"You'll soon find out. Trust me and do as I say." Swatting her backside, she yelped, and it served as a foreshadowing of things to come.

"That was uncalled for," she said, but did as she was told. He admired the view — her round bottom arched to him.

Moving to cover her body with his, he dragged a hand through her long hair to shift the length over one shoulder, baring her neck to him. He reached between her legs to feel the wetness already seeping from her core. Clearly, she'd enjoyed giving as much as he did receiving.

"So wet. You want this, don't you, sunshine?"

Her breathing hitched as he rubbed a finger over her pearl. "Yes, please. I've missed you."

"As my wife wishes."

Hazel panted into her pillow as he dropped a kiss to her bare shoulder before following the path of her spine with his lips.

"Jonathan..." She moaned, her fingers clutching the sheets underneath.

"Shh...relax."

"That may prove difficult if your mouth continues on its current path."

A teasing chuckle vibrated through his chest. "But it's such a delightful path," he said. Rough fingertips traced the crease between her raised bottom, and wicked ideas turned in his head like a carousel he saw once.

Save it for a later time.

Sliding further south, he reached his destination and rewarded himself with a swift jab of his tongue in her sheath. A high-pitched squeak briefly rent the air before becoming muffled as Hazel buried her head in the pillow. Pleased with the reaction, he copied the movement then switched to nibbling on her clitoris.

"Please...Oh, god." She rocked back against his teasing mouth, urging him to hurry. Ignoring her urgency, Jonathan continued leisurely licking through her folds, large hands cupping her bottom to keep her in place.

When the frequency of her moans increased, he knew she was on the precipice. Rearing back, he brought his eager cock to the junction of her thighs and plunged to the hilt in one smooth motion.

"Jonathan!" Fuck, how he loved hearing her scream his name. Keeping his pace deliberately controlled, he adjusted for the smallest response from her — intent on Hazel's pleasure.

This interlude would be an improvement over their first frenzied joining. She deserved to be cherished instead of roughly taken raw against the floor. Hard to regret it too much, though, when it gave him Hazel.

My wife.

Mine.

CHAPTER TWENTY-FOUR

H *e was torturing her.*
Hazel cried out again as Jonathan kept measured strokes instead of providing the relief she needed with a faster pace — a marked difference from their first meeting. But no less earth-shattering.

"Jonathan, please. Stop teasing me..."

"Now, why would I want to do that? Don't you enjoy feeling the drag of my cock along your quim? Each stroke aimed for your pleasure?" The sensual whisper heightened her awareness of him until she teetered on the edge of a precipice. He brushed against a sensitive spot inside, and her pleasure peaked in a burst of light.

She assumed he'd follow her into oblivion, but instead his thrusts became heavier, harsher. Fumbling for words, she mumbled, "What...?"

"Did you forget, sunshine? I'm of the rookery where we talk rough and fuck rougher. We're not done yet." She noticed he swore more when his passion was high, but it didn't bother her. In fact, it pleased her that she made him lose such control he could only express himself in the most base of ways.

He ravished her with each drive of his hips, and the bed shook with the aggressive movement. Calloused fingertips clenched around her hips, and she knew she'd bear bruises come morning — the idea of visible signs to show his passionate possession thrilling her. Hazel's muscles tensed before releasing in another engulfing orgasm as her core flexed around him, forcing Jonathan to finally join her in completion, his seed shooting inside before overflowing to her thighs.

Collapsing to the side, Hazel closed her eyes, heightening other sensations like the sound of their struggling breathing or the slow rasp as Jonathan separated their bodies only to wrap an arm around her from behind. The potent mix of lavender and rosemary became sharper from a sachet under her pillow.

"How are you feeling, sunshine?" Jonathan snuggled into her, his head burrowing into her neck.

"Like a proper wife," she said contentedly and snuggled into him. Exhaling a satisfied breath, she asked, "Why do you call me sunshine? I've been wondering for months now."

"Isn't it obvious? You're the light to my dark."

Maneuvering around to face him, she brushed a lock of hair off his forehead. "That's sweet, but you're too hard on yourself."

"And you always see the good in people."

"Not without reason. You may be in a precarious position as a member of a notorious gang, but I've never seen you as anything less than Peter's caring older brother. Your actions make up for any past or current perceived misdeeds." She prayed he'd listen and believe the declaration.

"I'm not so sure about that," he said and met her hopeful gaze. "Either way, that's why I call you sunshine. Do you dislike it?"

"Oh, no! Just a bit of curiosity." She enjoyed that he had a pet name for her. It made her feel special in his eyes.

"Speaking of curiosity, I didn't get to ask you earlier, but how did you feel about the wedding ceremony without your mother and father present? You weren't too sad?"

"A part of me regretted they weren't there, but for the most part, guilt overshadowed any sadness." The topic of the accident hadn't come up in detail between them before now, but she supposed it was time to share her greatest shame. No secrets between spouses and all that.

"Why would you feel guilt?"

Hazel mustered her courage, tension stiffening her shoulders. "Two years ago, my parents and I were travelling to Cheltham to see a visiting theater troupe. I'd persuaded them to take me as research for my own stories. My sisters weren't interested," she began after releasing a ragged breath. "It was a perfect summer day — sunny and warm." She remembered how excited she'd been, pelting Mama and Papa with question after question. "But as we crossed Shore Bridge, a loud cracking sounded and the bridge collapsed. Our carriage crashed into the dry creek beneath, shattered."

Jonathan stroked her arm, concern softening his gaze. "You must have been terrified."

"I don't know that I had enough time for terror. One moment I sat across from Mama and Papa, the next I lay pinned against the rocks by the wreckage." She pointed to her left shoulder. "That's where I got this scar. And why I reacted the way I did after my attack — the feeling of suffocating. Those attacks started after the accident whenever I'm overwhelmed or scared, then a numbness follows."

He traced the jagged line. "I'm glad you weren't hurt worse, though these attacks sound concerning. Have you seen a physician? Perhaps there's a way to rid yourself of the affliction."

She didn't respond, lowering her lashes to avoid his gaze. The worst of her confession was still to come.

"Hazel?"

"A doctor won't help, and I'm handling the episodes as they come. What matters is it should've been me instead of our parents who died."

"Don't say that."

"It's true. If you'd only known them, they were so smart, studying new plant species, working on groundbreaking research. They could have achieved so much more."

"That doesn't mean their lives were worth more than yours. They weren't the only ones able to accomplish great things. Look at your book and lessons," Jonathan said.

"My book's not published."

"Yet. It'll happen."

Hazel sighed. "Perhaps...But you see why I need to accomplish my goal of becoming an author. It's the one thread keeping me from falling into complete despair. If I can't make it work..."

"You will, but even if you don't, it won't mean your life is a waste. I hate that you've been thinking this way the entire time I've known you."

Forcing a brighter expression to her face, she appreciated the effort to comfort her, but the belief was too deeply embedded for him to simply dig out with a couple of kind words. And she didn't intend to spend her wedding night with him continuing to try. Changing the subject, she asked, "What about your parents?"

Jonathan turned onto his back, a short bark of laughter bursting from him, and she was grateful he seemed willing to switch topics. "I'm not sure my story's much better. They worked in one of the mills. Didn't care much for their children. My father approached me for money. Apparently, they thought I had a pile of cash lying around from my work with Lucien and wanted me to fund a move to a larger flat. I spurned him, and a week later the building collapsed, killing them."

"Oh, Jonathan! That's ghastly! Where was Peter?"

"Thankfully, Mrs. Wilson had taken Peter with her for a visit to her sister's, so they were safe. That's when her husband died as well."

"And the three of you became a family," she said, understanding dawning.

"I suppose so...But if it weren't for me, my parents may still live. I'd refused to loan the money. Where they lived was better than my own rundown room, better than where they lived when I grew up. Why waste money helping them move? I was selfish and greedy." Bitterness darkened his tone as his hand tightened on her waist.

"But you're not those things anymore," she said, caressing his cheek. "And you couldn't have known what would happen. It's not as if you caused the collapse."

"You're too quick to forgive me..." He murmured before groaning in disgust. "Aren't we a pair? Our wedding night, and we decided that swapping sad stories is the best way to spend our time."

Hazel laughed, allowing him to avoid the sore subject for the time being. "It is a touch melancholic." Rolling over, she propped herself up on his chest, leaning down for a kiss. "How about we change that? The night's still young."

Wrapping his arms around her, Jonathan smiled in agreement, and past memories faded away for another time.

THE NIGHT PASSED LIKE a dream Hazel never wanted to wake from — full of lovemaking and laughter — as she and Jonathan learned more about each other. However, dawn inevitably caught up to them, and she soon found herself waving goodbye to her family once again as they boarded the afternoon train to Manchester. Peter had left with Mrs. Wilson after the wedding, and upon their arrival to Devil's Haven, the couple was enveloped by their two missing compatriots.

Hazel wished they'd been able to enjoy a honeymoon after the wedding instead of rushing back to their duties, but she supposed such was the consequence of a hasty wedding prompted by scandal.

Tucking her empty valise in the wardrobe she now shared with Jonathan, a sense of home comforted her as she sank onto the end of the mattress and gazed around the room.

"Everything all right?" Jonathan asked after completing his own unpacking.

"Yes, I believe it is. Whatever comes next with Lucien or publishers, I know this is where I'm meant to be."

A smile softened his bearded face before he braced his arms on either side of her. "Something you've thought all along, if we're honest."

"True, though I'm glad you're finally on board with the prospect." That was one positive she hadn't considered: his warnings would finally cease.

"I accept that you belong with me and Pete. However, we're not staying in Devil's Haven, so I wouldn't get too comfortable."

"Fair point, dear husband." And her chin lifted for his kiss, warm contentment fluttering in her chest.

LIFE RETURNED TO NORMAL over the ensuing week as if they hadn't narrowly avoided scandal. She met Max, Jonathan's friend and business associate, and liked the large man despite the permanent scowl on his face. Her lessons resumed while Jonathan continued renovations, and after reading her novel to him, Peter, and Mrs. Wilson and hearing their praise, she worked up the courage to approach publishers again — this time in earnest.

So it was that she found herself approaching printer after printer that week — pitching her story — starting with her appointment at Steiner & Sons. Yet, despite the victory of achieving a meeting, she ultimately received a negative response. The resounding sound of "No" became a ringing in her ears as time after time, she received the same answer.

Approaching the small printer's office at the end of Market Street, she mustered her remaining well of courage and optimism, forcing a smile. This was the last address on her list.

I must make this work.

Walking through the door, a tinkling bell went off above her head, notifying everyone of her presence. A man with slicked hair and an ink-covered apron stepped forward. "May I help you, miss?"

"Good day, my name is Mrs. Hazel Travers, and I was hoping to speak with someone about publishing my children's book," she said in a rush.

Slow down. Act professional.

But each time she'd started speaking previously, it seemed like her time became shorter and shorter. She needed this man to hear her now, to possibly pique his interest.

The man looked her up and down. "I'm Mr. Willems, the owner of Willems Press, and I have some time to look it over now if you have it."

Excitement surged through her. This was the furthest she'd gotten. Pulling the pages out of her satchel, she handed it over to Mr. Willems. He laid it out on a counter and flipped through the pages so quickly, she questioned whether he was actually reading it or just making a show to appease her.

Finally, he turned the last page and gave the stack back to her. "I'm sorry. This isn't something we're interested in at this time. Thank you for stopping by."

"Oh. Is there something you didn't like? I'm open to making changes..."

"We don't have a market for fairy stories at the moment, and your sketches need work. Try reviewing Collins or Morris and you'll see what we're looking for. That's the caliber of work we publish," he said. "Now, if you'll excuse me, I need to return to my duties. Good day."

A crushing wave of numbness slammed into her at his dismissal — her last chance lost at sea. Then, like a ghost, she left, walking until she arrived home, unsure how she'd made it. All of her worst fears had been confirmed: she wasn't good enough. It wasn't about her being a woman. It was about her talent or lack thereof, and that stung worse. Prejudice because of sex she could handle but not the assertion that she wasn't a good enough writer or illustrator.

At least with the other publishers, it turned out to be a blessing they hadn't looked it over. They just shot her down flat. Yet, Mr. Willems had read it, been willing to take a chance, and she'd disappointed. Hurrying up the stairs to her room, she tripped over the last step as a watery haze blurred her vision. A cry burst out as she stumbled to her knees — whether in pain from the rejection or fall, she didn't know.

What was she going to do? What would she tell everyone?

They'd been supportive, but she knew their worries mounted each time she told of her losses. And now this — the final straw. Her sisters would know she failed just as they warned her. Jonathan would know she wasn't good enough and pity her, his poor wife.

"Mrs. Travers, is that you? Are you all right? I thought I heard something," Mrs. Wilson called out from the kitchen.

"I'm fine. I tripped over myself. So clumsy of me." She forced a laugh then bolted to her room and shut the door. Tossing her bag and a terrible excuse for a book to the floor, she crawled onto the bed and wondered what would happen to her now.

London was filled with publishers, but why would they be interested when smaller presses weren't? Her goal since arriving in Manchester had been to finish her book and get it published. She'd accomplished only one of those tasks with nothing to show for it.

I'm a failure, a talentless failure.

Mama and Papa would be so disappointed.

Tears soaked the coverlet beneath Hazel as admonishment after admonishment bombarded her. This wasn't supposed to happen. Why did fate save her over her parents only to have her fail?

CHAPTER TWENTY-FIVE

"A married man...I still can't believe it." Max shook his head in disbelief as they trekked back to Jonathan's home carrying more buckets of paint to finish the third floor. The familiar refrain amused him — it echoed his own incredulity at the recent turn of his life.

"Join the club," he said. "But married life isn't the ball and chain you imagine. Hazel supports this boarding house scheme, believes in me more than I do myself."

"I'll admit you found one of the good ones."

Jonathan laughed. "I suppose I should be grateful she's so stubborn and ignored my warnings about Devil's Haven."

They entered the front door and headed upstairs when he heard something sounding suspiciously like crying coming from behind his bedroom door. Setting his load down, he waved Max to continue on without him. "Thanks for your help. I'll catch up with you later."

Max cast a worried gaze towards the door and nodded in understanding. Knocking softly, Jonathan crossed the threshold to find Hazel laying face-down on the counterpane, cheeks streaked with tears.

Another sob erupted, her body shaking in despair. He shut the door and climbed onto the bed beside her. "Hazel, love, what's wrong?" An inkling of what it could be sat in his gut —

she'd visited her last round of publishers today, and this didn't bode well for her results.

"It's over." She hiccuped. "It's all over." Then she relayed the latest rejections she'd received that day. Unsure what to do, he pressed closer and wrapped an arm around her body, cupping one of her hands.

"This isn't the end. We can't let one town of incompetent printing presses derail your dream. We'll keep searching, and if no one's smart enough to publish your book, we'll do it ourselves," he said, a fuzzy plan forming. He'd make it happen for Hazel — no matter the cost.

She gave a watery laugh. "That's sweet of you to say, but we don't have that kind of money."

"I've been saving for years with key investments along with my wages from Lucien. To be truthful, if I weren't such a coward, the money probably would've been enough for me to sever ties from him earlier. But if it's not enough to publish your book, I can take on more work for the Cobblewallers. How much can printing cost?"

A small fortune. But her success and happiness trumped finances.

She turned over, alarm on her face, and placed a hand on his cheek. "Oh no! You mustn't do that. That money is for your dream and this building — to get away from Lucien, not get bound tighter in his web. I couldn't bear it if I took that away from you."

"Nonsense. What's mine is yours. You wouldn't be taking anything I wasn't willing to give anyway."

"Jonathan, no. I feel guilty enough already." A fresh wave of tears welled up in her eyes. "This was supposed to be my calling

— the reason I was worth saving over my parents — to become an acclaimed author for children. To prove it wasn't all a waste."

A frown wrinkled his brow. "What will it take for you to understand that's not true?"

Squeezing his arm in desperation, a panicked flare took over her expression. "Don't you see? All my life I've been the head-in-the-clouds dreamer daughter — coddled and encouraged in my creative pursuits — but never taken seriously. No one truly believed I was capable of caring for myself or accomplishing much outside a potential marriage. And I've proven them right." She covered a short gasp with a trembling hand. "But if my parents had survived in my place, think of all they would've done, the important scientific discoveries. My sisters would still have Mama and Papa instead of me — the trouble-causing, worry-inducing baby sister."

She felt so strongly about the connection between the accident, her parents, and her book. How could he combat the false correlation?

An underlying bleakness tainted her unflappable ambition. After her confession on their wedding night, he'd realized the emotion ran deeply inside her, and guilt had slid down his spine at not noticing earlier. Perhaps he could've saved her some misplaced heartache instead of being selfishly immersed in his own problems.

Like you're saving her from pain now?

"Your life is worth more than a book — worth more than anything you could possibly do. It's priceless," he said, rubbing soothing circles over her back, determined to help her see reason. "Do you think I should've perished in that building collapse instead of my mother and father? Would Pete be better off?"

"No, of course not. That's not what I'm —"

"I admit to a measure of guilt for not providing aid when they asked, but I don't feel guilty for surviving. Bad things happen all the time; it's no one's fault. Your survival doesn't sentence you to a life of justifying the decision. That's no way to live." The words came from deep inside him and penetrated his own portion of guilt and shame. More and more, he realized how similar he and Hazel were, but it wasn't until these moments when forced to offer comfort for her that he found the same.

She didn't reply, clearly not ready to accept that truth.

Well, if words can't help...

"If you need to forget for a while, let me take your mind off things for a few hours." He brushed a tentative kiss over the back of her neck, seeking approval.

She stiffened at the contact. "Is it okay if we don't make love?" Her weak whisper broke his heart while simultaneously kicking him in the gut. What more could he do to make her feel better? As if she heard his unspoken question, she asked, "Can you just hold me, please?"

"Of course, love." Tightening his grip, he curved his body further around hers to form a cocoon of protection. This was all new to him: comforting a woman. Yet Hazel was his wife now. It was his duty to care for her needs — physical and emotional. It may prove that he had no skill for such tasks, but he'd try for her.

CHAPTER TWENTY-SIX

"Perfect, Mary." Hazel patted the girl's back as she buried the tiny seeds in one of the dirt-filled pots lining the wall. The rest of the children sat in various stages of the same task while she supervised to make sure things didn't get too out of hand. Peter knelt helping another little girl, and Hazel smiled at the sight.

Such a sweet boy. Like his brother.

After a string of miserable days, she'd decided to kill two birds with one stone: spruce up the utilitarian room and cheer her up in the process. Gardening reminded her of time spent with Mama, learning about a seed's growth cycle, and seeing the fruits of their labor over time. And she figured it'd be a nice hiatus from reading.

"Remember to bury the seeds a finger deep." She held up a finger to demonstrate. "If it's too close to the surface, the roots won't have enough soil to grow."

"My, what an industrious little bunch you have here, Mrs. Travers." An unfamiliar voice interrupted their lesson as a red-haired woman and Dot stood by the doorway.

Walking forward to greet the newcomer, she wiped her dirty hands on the apron around her waist. "Good afternoon, and yes, we're all quite excited about today's assignment."

"Hazel, this is Mrs. Johanna Forrester, Dr. Forrester's wife. I believe you've met him a couple of times. Johanna and I became friends a while back, and when she inquired about your charity work here, I knew the two of you needed to meet," Dot said, gesturing between the two women.

"Oh, of course! Your husband's been most helpful with the children when we've gotten into scrapes. Is there anything in particular you'd like to know more about?" Hazel thought it strange someone took interest in her lessons with the children, but who was she to judge?

"You teach reading and science. Can I assume there's also a maths portion of study? I find it fascinating how you've taken a weekly book club and transformed it into a miniature school for those who can't afford the local elementary. It's quite admirable." Mrs. Forrester smiled, her green eyes sparkling, and Hazel felt a twitch of resentment at the praise.

"I'm not a teacher. This isn't a school." Perhaps more blunt than polite, but she didn't want to hear how great everyone thought the class was, as if it should be what she wanted to do with her life. It was meant to be charity, not her life's ambition. And it was too soon to consider the transition with the wound of publishers' rejections so fresh.

Your life's ambition failed, remember?

Mrs. Forrester looked taken aback by her tone, and Dot tried to smooth over the awkward moment. "We understand. It's just amazing how far you've taken your responsibility to the children. You have a real knack for teaching, and we thought you should know how impressive all of this is."

"I apologize for snapping." She brought a hand to her forehead. "I'm not myself today. Please join us. We have plenty of seeds, dirt, and pots — enough for everyone."

Hazel picked up spare aprons for the women, and they enjoyed chatting about Mrs. Forrester's adventures in Devil's Haven when she accompanied her husband on patient calls.

"What an enterprising woman you are, Mrs. Forrester. How fortunate you were to find your purpose and true love tied together in one."

"Well, it didn't start out that way...I thought I'd be a wife and mother with my first husband, only to be widowed and childless years later. Then, I discovered a new path to those things along with exploring my passion for aiding those in need." Mrs. Forrester patted the dirt in her pot to form a smooth surface. "But sometimes the path we expect isn't always best or what's needed."

"Something to think about," Dot murmured, her meaning no great mystery.

Hazel forced a smile and nodded in agreement — unwilling to continue the earlier conversation. Each time the subject came up, whether by Dot or Jonathan, tiny pin pricks like needles piercing her skin ran along her body, deflating her a bit more until she feared there'd be nothing left.

Maybe someday the thought wouldn't hurt so much, until then she wished people would let her grieve the loss of her dream.

"On a happier note, how is married life? I must confess to quite a shock upon receiving your letter." Hazel imagined her friend would be surprised considering how little she'd mentioned Jonathan in their previous conversations. Thankful for the turn of topic, the women chatted about marriage and Dot's future with a handsome young curate while helping the children finish planting their seeds.

AFTER THE CHILDREN, Mrs. Forrester, and Dot left an hour later, she heard Jonathan knocking about upstairs. He must've woken from his nap and gotten straight to work assuming she still had class. A flicker of insecurity went off inside at his absence. Since their marriage, he hadn't stayed for many lessons like he used to, and she wondered if he began to tire of her.

Don't be ridiculous.

Jonathan seemed as devoted as ever, though, never voicing his true feelings. And as a wordsmith that loss bothered her. *It's not like you've told him such things either.*

Standing in the empty room with the effects of the past week hanging over her, she decided she could use some husbandly comfort — and proof that his interest remained with her, no matter the illogical doubts that popped up when she felt so low.

The sound of hammering became louder the higher Hazel climbed, rarely venturing this far — the fourth floor — as he always insisted it wasn't ready for anyone but him to see. Yet, the further she walked the more confused she became. Why did he insist the building wasn't ready for tenants to move in when the fresh wallpaper and fixtures gleamed?

Leaning against the open doorway at the end of the hall, Hazel's breath stuck in her throat at the vision Jonathan made. An unbuttoned shirt stuck to his sweat, making it sheer and drawing her closer. She must have made a sound because he turned towards her in surprise, revealing more of his bare chest.

"How did the children enjoy their lesson today?" he asked, pulling a worn rag tucked at his waist and swiping it over his forehead and the back of his neck.

"Everyone loved it," she said distractedly. Itching to touch him, she glided a hand inside the open collar. "Do you remember when you asked if I wanted you to help me forget?"

"Yes..."

"I do now." She met his lustful eyes, their breathing turning hard, hot.

"Undo my trousers," he ordered, his firm voice sending a shiver down her spine. Removing the closure, Hazel reached in and tentatively stroked him while he rucked up her skirts and brought his hand to the slit of her drawers. "You're wet all ready."

"Because you look delicious. I want to lick you up." The explicit words ignited more fire between them.

"Are you trying to talk dirty to me?"

"You say stuff like that all the time, so I thought I'd try. Was it okay?"

He grinned. "Say what you want, little wanton."

Returning the smile, she continued to stroke him. "Here, let me make things a little easier." Jonathan took her palm and brought it to her own sex.

"Jonathan..." A hot blush ran across her skin along with another rush of arousal at the naughty act. Together they rubbed between her thighs until the evidence of her desire coated her palm. Satisfied with his handiwork, he brought her hand back to his engorged member and imitated how he wanted her to pump him.

Their eyes locked as he returned his hand to her body — pleasuring each other. Nothing else touched, just their hands making sloppy wet sounds. All the communication they needed occurred in their gazes.

Her need for a reprieve from melancholic thoughts.

His desire to provide such relief.

Too soon their movements quickened, and their mutual cries of satisfaction echoed in the otherwise empty room. Sinking to the floor, Hazel collapsed against Jonathan as he nuzzled her cheek.

"Thank you," she whispered and closed her eyes, drifting in the blissful afterglow.

"Any time, sunshine. Whenever you need me, I'll be here."

As declarations go, she'd accept whatever he gave her.

CHAPTER TWENTY-SEVEN

"Cara! What are you doing here?" Hazel motioned for her sister to come in, noting the travel bag in hand.

"I thought I'd take my cue from you and leave Hampshire for a bit. It's been so long," Caraway said, moving further down the hall inspecting the walls and framed paintings Hazel had added until stopping at the classroom. "Is this where you teach the children?"

"Yes, Jonathan installed the new blackboard, and soon we'll have long tables for the children to work on." Hazel came up behind her sister and leaned against the doorjamb, proud of how far the room had come since Jonathan had first offered it to her. No longer did it lay empty. Benches, books, and drawings filled the area.

"How lovely. I'm impressed you've chosen to undertake teaching while trying to publish your book. I suppose that's a bit of Papa in you — always so industrious."

Sadness washed through her at the comparison, although strangely the guilt she usually felt wasn't as strong. Perhaps her talk with Jonathan had helped after all.

"Well, I'm not sure if writing's what I'm meant to do with my life considering recent events."

Caraway whipped her head around in shock. "What? The whole reason you're here is because of your writing. What's changed?"

Hazel sighed as she recalled the last rejection she received. "Come on. Let's get you settled. I'm assuming you're staying with us for the duration of your stay?"

"If that's all right. I know it's rude that I didn't notify you first, but it was a bit of a spur-of-the-moment decision."

"Of course, it's fine. Thankfully, Jonathan has a couple of finished rooms for you to choose from upstairs. Afterwards, we'll have some tea, and we can talk."

A quarter of an hour later, they sat at the kitchen table where Mrs. Wilson set out biscuits with tea. "Thank you, Mrs. Wilson."

"It's my pleasure. You two enjoy catching up." She patted Hazel on the shoulder and left them alone. Unable to put it off any longer, Hazel launched into the events of the past few weeks including her visit to Black Press.

"Oh, that sounds horrendous. I'm so sorry, dear." Caraway reached a hand across the table to clasp her own. "What will you do now?"

"I've been thinking about focusing on teaching more. It appears I may have a talent for it. At least that's what people keep telling me," she said, trying to force optimism into her tone to match her words. "My writing will always be there, and I'll continue to pursue it. But more and more, I'm realizing that I've placed a timeline on myself that isn't very realistic."

Caraway sat back and took a sip of tea. "Well, that is certainly a change."

"Don't tell me you disapprove of this new path, as well," Hazel said in surprise. Would she never do right in the eyes of her sister?

"No, no...I think this is an excellent plan. You've always had a connection with children — something about your creative whimsy helps you relate to them better. It makes sense that you would find fulfillment through teaching." Caraway stared off to the side, a contemplative look on her face.

"Yet something's bothering you."

"It's not you." Caraway exhaled a heavy breath and traced the grain on the kitchen table before meeting Hazel's inquisitive gaze. "I'm proud of all you've accomplished even if I haven't always shown it. The fact of the matter is... I've been jealous."

"What? Why?"

Caraway faced her more fully, a grim smile lifting her mouth. "Do you remember that time we performed your play for Mama and Papa? You wrote this fantastical story about pirates and mermaids, and we spent weeks creating costumes. You've always known what you wanted to do, who you wanted to be — even if it wasn't until recently that you struck out to achieve it. I admire and envy that about you."

"But you could do the same thing," Hazel said. Her sister's confession surprised her. She assumed Caraway was happy staying in Hampshire. Content to wait for marriage and family to come along.

"Oh, Hazel." Caraway patted her hand. "I've never felt a strong pull towards any sort of direction. I expected to marry when it was time, but I'm afraid that dream may be coming to an end. I'm six and twenty, unmarried, stuck in our country cottage." She wiped at a lone tear and shook her head.

"Don't worry, I'll help you. Together we'll figure out something."

"We'll see," Caraway said, doubt clear in her voice. But Hazel was determined. If she could leave home and thrive so could Caraway. She was practical, responsible — her talents could be put to use anywhere. They just had to find the right fit.

And selfishly, it comforted her a bit to know that Caraway's resistance to her writing dream had little to do with her actual belief in Hazel. "All this time, I felt like you didn't believe in me, that I was wasting my life — wasting the chance fate handed me when I survived the accident and not Mama and Papa."

"I apologize that it came off that way. I didn't mean to hurt you. And don't be mistaken: there were some doubts but not because I didn't think you were talented enough. It's a harsh world for women, and I wanted to protect you from it." She took another sip of tea before shaking her head in incredulity. "You're certainly not wasting your life. Look at all you've done in such a short period of time!"

"Yes, but Mama and Papa would've done so much more," she said morosely. Feeling the weight of their lives on her shoulders.

"Perhaps, but it doesn't mean that you should've died in their places. Honestly, Hazel, sometimes I fear for how dramatically your mind conjures situations," Caraway huffed, her mouth thinning in disapproval. "Don't you remember how often their papers got rejected? Especially Mama's as she was only Papa's assistant. Did that mean her worth was any less?" She didn't wait for Hazel's response. "No, it doesn't. And your recent rejection doesn't mean that either. It's just not time yet. Probably because you're meant to teach, which when you think about it is a full circle moment — improving students' minds like Papa used to."

For some reason, Hazel hadn't made that connection before. Oh, she'd considered how her father had been a professor, but he'd gone to university and studied while she had no formal education beyond what her parents taught her.

Which may be formal enough...

Caraway was right. She'd tied so much of her identity into being an author — disparaging the thought of settling for teaching — when her parents might very well approve of such a profession for their daughter. Maybe she should start considering it more seriously with an eye for positivity, instead of faking a happy demeanor with the change to her plans.

And she didn't have to stop writing. In fact, she could test stories with the children — her ideal audience.

"I hadn't thought of it like that..."

"Of course not. Once you've set your mind to one course, you can be very stubborn."

"Truer words were never spoken. I speak from firsthand experience," Jonathan said as he entered the kitchen. "What a welcome surprise to see you again, Miss Taylor."

"We're in-laws now. You can call me Caraway or Cara, and I'm glad we're agreed on Hazel's temperament when it comes to certain ideas."

"Now, wait a minute..." The conversation moved onto a friendly gibing session at her expense, but Hazel appreciated watching Jonathan and Caraway bond over a mutual mission.

And it lent her a reprieve to process the new perspective she'd gotten from Caraway. For the first time in a while, a modicum of joy for her future broke through some of the cracks in her heart.

CHAPTER TWENTY-EIGHT

"Consider this my notice," Jonathan said as he tossed the last purse of coins on Lucien's desk.

"Notice, eh? I thought we already had this discussion: you're not free until I say so."

"This is the last collection I'll be making. There's nothing else tying me to you, and I've expressed my gratitude before for your help." Jonathan swallowed a bit of bile at the sucking up he had to do, but he wanted to make this break as easy as possible in the hopes that Lucien wouldn't retaliate. "But it's time for me to move on, and you'll be free to promote someone else. I think Martin would be interested." He named a man who'd been eyeing his position for some time now — eager to get in good with the boss.

"But I'm not. You're the man for the job. You've just married; if it's time you need with your little ladybird, take it. I'm not so unreasonable that I'll stand in the way of a man tupping his wife," Lucien said, starting to jot notes down on the ledger in front of him as if this conversation wasn't worth his time. "When you return, you'll be refreshed, and there will be no more talk of leaving."

"No."

The pen skittered to a halt. Looking up slowly, Lucien repeated the word. "No?"

"I'm done. Find another lackey. And until you do, Max is more than capable of handling your clients." Jonathan held his arms loosely at his sides, in case Lucien motioned for his guard to attack to prove his point. Oliver stood in the background, silent and unobtrusive, waiting for his master's call.

"You don't know what you're doing. You don't want to make an enemy of me."

"I don't harbor any animosity towards you. Let's part friends and leave it at that. Goodbye, Lucien." He tipped his head and exited, keeping an even step, not too fast or slow to showcase possible weakness or fear.

Once he made it safely outside, he took a grateful breath. He doubted that would be the end with Lucien, but he'd deal with that conversation later. For now, he was free, and he couldn't wait to tell Hazel. She'd been encouraging him to take this step, to finally commit to the boarding house, and he'd done it.

"I see you're still in one piece," Max said from his perch on an overturned bin. He didn't like spending any more time inside the den than necessary and waited for the outcome of Jonathan's decree outside.

"For the moment," Jonathan agreed, taking another deep breath. It might be full of the rank smell of the alley, but he didn't care because the high coursing through his blood couldn't be tamed. "Keep me apprised of anything you hear about possible blowback, would you?"

Max nodded before clasping his shoulder firmly in a gesture of encouragement. "I've got your back, though soon I'm hoping to make my own break for it."

"If you're interested in the hospitality business..." Jonathan raised his hands suggestively. He didn't know how Max could fit in at the boarding house, but he wouldn't leave a friend in need.

"I'll leave that to you and Mrs. Travers." Max stepped back and dipped his head. "Enjoy your freedom. We'll speak later."

Turning around, Jonathan started the walk home, and a slight smile formed on his face at the way his life was turning out. He had a beautiful wife who believed in him, and soon he'd be a legitimate business owner. What more could he want?

"I DID IT." JONATHAN came up behind Hazel as she finished brushing her hair before bed.

"Did what?"

"Quit. I told Lucien tonight was my last night."

Her eyes widened, and she set the brush down before turning around to face him on the small bench in front of the vanity. Placing her hands on his waist, she looked up to meet his eyes. "How did he handle it?"

"Not well, but I'll take it as a good sign that he let me leave unharmed." He stroked a hand down one of her curls — tugging then letting it loose to spring back into form.

"Thank God for small mercies! I'm so proud of you. I knew you could do it," she said, squeezing his hips.

"All because of you. Without your support, who knows how much longer it would've taken me to make the leap? I should thank you." His eyes beckoned in desire as she understood his meaning.

"I was actually thinking I could reward you." She licked her lips, drawing his gaze to the pink bow.

"Oh? And what did you have in mind?"

She played with the buttons of his trousers before answering. "Kissing you...here." Her hand cupped him through the thin fabric, his erection already growing at the explicit suggestion.

"You want to take me in your mouth? As a reward?"

"Yes." She hesitated briefly before lowering her head in assent. "You deserve it, and I enjoy doing this for you."

"How could I refuse you?" Lowering his hands to her shoulders, he said, "Your wish is my command. Do as you will, dear wife."

Biting her lip, she eyed the front placket and carefully released the buttons so the flaps fell open and his cock sprang free. Leaning forward, she brushed a kiss over the mushroom head, coming away a bit wet from the tip.

Jonathan groaned after she licked it away. Trying again, she wrapped a hand around his base, holding him still so she could place pursed lips over the top and sucked lightly.

"Harder, sunshine," Jonathan instructed. Following his orders, she opened wider and let him slide further in her mouth until he butted up against the back of her throat. Coughing a little, she jerked back, red heat covering her cheeks in embarrassment.

"I'm sorry. I didn't mean to do that."

He cupped the back of her head and, gently, said, "It's okay. You're doing fine. And we can stop at any time. Just go slow; you'll adjust to it. Remember the cottage."

The memory of the first and only time she'd done this made him burn to take control, but he held off. Trusting him, she repeated the movement. This time when he touched her throat, her tongue pushed up underneath, and she sucked hard like he said as she pulled back until releasing him with a loud sucking noise.

"Like that, right?"

His breathing became ragged, but he answered. "Perfect. Now, keep doing that, bobbing up and down as if I was fucking your cunt instead of your mouth."

The crude words were harsh, but he saw the way she squeezed her thighs together in response. *Soon*. But first, she was seeing to his pleasure. *Rewarding him*. Lowering her head, she suckled him deeper and harder, following each retreat with her hand to make sure he was always being held until he tugged on the back of her head.

"Sunshine. I'm about to...*Christ*!" His cock throbbed in her mouth pumping his spend down her throat as she kept swallowing it, until he finally pulled away.

Helping her up, Jonathan buried his head in her neck, holding her tightly to him as his heart pounded rapidly against her chest. Soothing circles smoothed over his back.

"I take it you enjoyed that?" she asked smugly, clearly proud of what she'd done.

"Immensely. You're going to be the death of me."

"I hope not. I was hoping to continue your reward on the bed."

He laughed and lifted his head. Brushing a kiss over her swollen lips, he nodded. "Like I said, your wish is my command." And proceeded to follow through on his promise for the rest of the evening.

CARAWAY'S LAST FULL day with the Travers family dawned frigid and rainy — perfect for spending the day indoors. Gathered around the kitchen table, they surveyed the bits of lace, ribbon, silk flowers, and various accoutrements with varying degrees of excitement. With Valentine's Day arriving soon, Hazel had thought it'd be fun to create valentines as a family activity.

Jonathan held up a long red ribbon, gingerly pinching it between thumb and forefinger. "What exactly are we supposed to do with these?"

"Design a valentine. Don't you want to *Be Mine*?" She found the clichéd clipping with the words printed elaborately in scrolling font and waved it playfully in the air.

"I have a marriage certificate to prove I already am," he said in rebuttal.

"Children, children..." Caraway clucked her tongue, stepping into the role of peacekeeper — something Jonathan had realized was a usual occurrence for her. "*Be Mine* isn't in question. It's the *Constant and True* we should be concerned about." She showcased another little saying.

He almost offered an argument for the insult until the sparkle in his sister-in-law's eyes revealed she was only teasing.

"I'm going to come up with my own saying," Pete said and reached across the table gathering white lace and pink flowers.

"Smart move, lad. And who will receive such a masterpiece?" The three adults observed the hot flush creeping up the boy's cheeks and grinned at the display. It seemed his little brother had a crush.

"No one. I'm only making one because I have to," he mumbled, staring down at the decorations in his hands. Jonathan leaned over to ruffle the boy's hair.

"Fine, keep your secrets. But I'm looking forward to the inscription — curious to see how much of Hazel's writing talents have rubbed off on you."

Hazel gave a self-deprecating laugh. "Yes, that will be interesting to see..."

"You know, she used to write the most bombastic poems for valentines," Caraway said. Arranging a group of purple silk flowers in one corner of her card, she began gluing them down.

"I'd forgotten about those. It's been so long since we've done valentines."

Better than him. He'd never made one before, hadn't really had a reason to until now.

"Which is why I'm glad you suggested we make these today. I can carry Iris's and Lily's home with me to save on postage." Leave it to Caraway to care about such a practical concern — another characteristic he'd noticed from Hazel's eldest sister.

"Perhaps I'll hide mine," Jonathan said, attempting to detach a sticky piece of lace from his hand by shaking it. "Make it more of a treasure hunt than placing it on your pillow or something so trivial."

"Oh, I like that plan." Hazel's eyes sparkled in glee as elegant swoops became letters on her valentine.

"Like Easter!" Pete chimed in.

A sense of contentment bloomed inside Jonathan as the chatter continued around him. Such a domestic scene never would have happened if it weren't for Hazel. His wife made this place a home. Something he and Pete had desperately needed even if they hadn't realized it.

The depth of his emotions for his wife scared the hell out of him which is why he hadn't been able to put them into words. Perhaps this little valentine could serve a purpose, after all — expressing his feelings without giving him the opportunity to fumble by speaking. And curiosity nipped at him as he wondered if Hazel's card to him would do the same.

She'd kept her own sentiments close to the chest, and it rubbed.

Hypocrite.

He wanted to hear her say the words first.

Coward.

But eventually, someone would have to break that particular silence. He only hoped they both heard mutual proclamations.

CHAPTER TWENTY-NINE

Aweek later, on Valentine's Day, the children passed around the cards they'd made. After having such a successful afternoon with the family, Hazel thought it would make a fun activity for the children, and she was right. Cara's visit had proved beneficial in more than one way in the end.

"This is for you, Mrs. Travers." The little girl held out a folded card with haphazard hearts drawn on the front.

"Thank you, Mary. How thoughtful!" Opening it to read the inside, a rush of tears welled up as the words pierced her heart.

Dear Mrs. Travers,
I hope I spelled that right. You are my favorite teacher.
Love, Mary

The painstaking scrawl featured no mistakes and proved how much the children had learned.

I am an utter fool.

Despite constant hints and a facade of pretending, she finally recognized herself as an educator, and it was something to be proud of — not look down upon as a lesser profession from her original goal. The depth of her delusion knocked the breath from her, and she placed a steadying hand on the desk behind her.

"This is lovely, and you spelled everything correctly."

The girl's smile brightened her skinny face before she ran off to another group of little girls espousing her success. Caressing the words on the card, Hazel admonished her stubbornness even as she shed the heaviness she'd been toting around. Teaching wasn't a compromise. It wasn't a less noble profession than writing. And her worth didn't come from it.

Finally, she accepted what everyone had been telling her all this time — a decision that was quite easy to make once she'd chosen to loosen her grip on the past. The accident had left an indelible mark on her, but she'd no longer live life guilty for surviving. It's not what her parents would have wanted, and it's not what her family needed.

A burst of energy propelled her to move to the blackboard, needing to do something and wishing Jonathan were present so she could share her revelation. Instead, Hazel erased the Valentine's sayings she'd written on the board until the excited chatter in the room abruptly stopped.

An eerie silence fell over the room, and a chill worked its way up Hazel's spine. Turning around slowly, she saw the cause for the sudden quiet — three men stood in the back of the room blocking the door and their only way out.

She recognized the large one on the right as Max, a frequent associate of Jonathan on his nighttime runs, and a friend...or so she thought. Now she wasn't so sure.

"Children, come here." She eyed the men warily as the children moved to do her bidding. "May I help you, gentlemen?"

"So, you're the little baggage that's causing trouble." The man in the middle stepped forward as his beady eyes took in the room.

"I'm not sure what you mean, sir. I don't believe we've ever met."

"The name's Amos Lucien. Perhaps you've heard of me. Your husband worked for me before deciding he'd be better off striking out on his own. Sound familiar?"

"Jonathan's not here at the moment, but I'll be sure to let him know you stopped by." Hazel felt Peter and Mary scoot closer, their hands clinging tightly to her skirts. The air in the room became thin as the tell-tale stuttering of her lungs heralded an oncoming attack.

No, you mustn't give in. The children need you.

Counting her breaths, Hazel focused on staying in control instead of succumbing to the usual routine of labored breathing then numbness.

"Ah, but it's you I've come to see. You're the problem, ever since you started traipsing around Devil's Haven." Lucien reached into his jacket and pulled out a pistol, the light filtering in through the window glinting off the metal barrel. Her eyes widened in shock as she tried to shuffle the children further behind her, though it was impossible to provide a barrier for all of them.

"The way I see it," he continued. "I've lost one of my best men because of you. He needs to be reminded who runs this part of town. No one leaves the Cobblewallers without my permission or else." He raised the pistol to point it at her chest. The breath froze in her lungs, and she wondered if she'd survived everything in her past just to die by the hand of a notorious gang leader.

"Harming me won't bring Jonathan back to you."

"This isn't about bringing him back. It's about keeping him and everyone else in Devil's Haven in line. If someone crosses me, there are consequences," Lucien said.

She noticed Max take a step closer while the other man remained to block the doorway.

"At least let the children go. They have nothing to do with this, and I'm not sure the people of Devil's Haven will look kindly on you harming innocents."

Lucien mulled the idea over before motioning with his pistol. "I'm not a monster. I can be very generous when needed. Run along little ones before I change my mind."

Hazel hated how unprotected the children would be walking past the deranged man, but her skirts would only provide so much protection if they stayed behind her. She was surprised at how easily Lucien capitulated to her request, though she wouldn't look a gift horse in the mouth.

Peter squeezed her arm, and she worried he might try to stay out of loyalty until he kept walking, an arm around Mary. With the children distracting the men, Hazel groped backwards for her satchel and Papa's pistol. Hands touched worn leather, and she carefully slid it closer, hiding her movements within her skirts.

Time to prove your mettle.

"JON!" MRS. WILSON HURRIED towards him, almost tripping over the skirts whipping around her legs. He'd left to secure permits to officially open the boarding house, and he'd been looking forward to telling Hazel of his success.

"Mrs. Wilson, what's wrong?"

"Lucien. He interrupted class. I don't know what he's up to, but it can't be good." The words were rushed, out of breath, but he understood them well enough. Fear tickled the back of his neck.

Hazel. Pete. The rest of the children. They were all in danger.

"Tell me everything."

She told him how she'd been in the kitchen at the back of the building when she heard a commotion and saw Lucien, Max, and another man enter the classroom. Sneaking out the back exit, Mrs. Wilson had been able to escape undetected. And a rush of gratitude bombarded him at her luck.

Once she'd finished, he took off on a run — dodging people on the streets — until he reached home. This was all his fault. He'd put his family at risk by keeping them in such close quarters to Lucien. Everything he'd feared was coming to pass.

Looking around the outside of the boarding house, he tried to figure out what to do when a line of children exited the building.

But no Hazel.

"Pete, are you all right? Where's Hazel?" Jonathan grabbed his brother by his arms, pulling him to the opposite side of the street as the rest of the children congregated around him, crying and gibbering at once. "It's going to be okay. You're safe now, and soon Miss Taylor will be, too."

"You've got to help her. Lucien's got a gun!" Pete's voice wobbled as tears shone in his eyes, and Jonathan swore his former boss would pay.

Glaring at the front of his home, a plan formed in his mind. "Pete, here's what we're going to do." After relaying his plan, they got into position with him crouched low and creeping up to the front entry. He gave the go-ahead with a nod of his head, and a rock sailed through the air into the classroom's glass window, shattering it on impact and, hopefully, providing enough of a distraction for Jonathan to get inside.

Bursting through the doorway, he found Oliver blocking the entry to the class with Max's arm wrapped around his neck.

The man clawed at his arm, trying to get free, but Max held tight. Jonathan knew he could count on his friend to have his back.

Scanning the room, he found Hazel trapped at the front of the room, that damned pistol shaking in her hands as Lucien had his own gun trained on her.

"Give it up, Lucien. Leave now before someone gets hurt," he warned, matching Lucien's steps as the crime lord maneuvered around the room keeping Hazel and Jonathan within sight.

"Your ladybird won't shoot. She's a *lady*." The derisive tone dripped with sarcasm.

"I wouldn't be so sure," Hazel said, and Jonathan watched a transformation strengthen her posture and grip. A shout of fear stuck in his throat when a gunshot boomed through the room.

A few of the lingering children screamed outside, but his focus was on the sudden warrior woman his wife had become. Shock painted her face as the pistol fell to her side, and he immediately tackled Lucien who stood moaning, a hand to his bleeding shoulder, though his gun still loomed large.

"She shot me! Your bloody wife shot me!" Lucien tried aiming for Jonathan, their fighting forms rolling on the ground until another shot rang out, a feminine cry of terror erupting from Hazel. Heart beating out of his chest, Jonathan took stock of his limbs.

Everything seemed to be in working order, but it appeared the same could not be said for Lucien — his prone body lying lifeless on top of Jonathan's.

"Jonathan! Are you hurt?" Hazel fell to his side, frantic hands running along the parts of him she could reach under Lucien's heavy mass.

"I think so. The pistol turned on him and accidentally fired. Is he really dead?"

Max knelt on his other side and pressed two fingers to Lucien's bulging neck, searching for a pulse but finding none with a negative shake of his head, and a weight lifted from Jonathan's shoulders as elation coursed through him. No longer would Lucien be hanging over his head.

Free.

"Yes." Their eyes met, and he could read the reciprocating relief in Max's eyes. They were both free.

"Good riddance then," Max said, rolling the dead man off Jonathan. "I'll deal with Oliver before helping you dispose of the body. The rookery's going to be up in arms when this gets out."

"Thank you for your help, Max," he said before Hazel wrapped her arms around his neck.

"I'm so happy you're safe. What were you thinking jumping on him like that?"

"Me? You're the one who shot him. He could've returned the fire if you missed." A vision of her cold and lifeless sent him into a dark abyss he never wanted to frequent again.

"But I didn't miss." Her lips buried in his hair, needing to be as close as possible. "It's finally over. We don't have to worry about him anymore."

"I know, sunshine. I know." Stroking her hair, he saw blood spreading from the wound in Lucien's chest. "But Max and I need to deal with the body while you see to the children. They're outside frightened out of their minds."

"You're right, of course." Reluctantly letting him go, they both got to their feet. "Frankly, I'm still shaken, too. You could've been killed."

Pulling off his jacket, he placed it over the body, covering Lucien's face and the blood. "The same goes for you, sunshine, but thank god, I got here in time. Now, look after the children. I won't be long."

Hazel scurried away, and Jonathan shook his head, resolved to make sure any reminders of their ordeal was wiped clean from the room before she returned. Sighing, he and Max worked together to erase the presence of Lucien while Mrs. Wilson appeared with a bucket of soap and water along with rags to scrub the blood from the floorboards. After dumping Lucien's body in an unmarked grave at the edge of town, he took a moment to observe Mrs. Wilson's cleaning once home again — the sounds of the bristles on her brush scratching against the floor.

"I'm glad you made it out safely to warn me, Mrs. Wilson. Thank you again," he said softly.

"We're fortunate that the fool thought so highly of himself. Coming through the front door, brazen as you please, instead of breaking in through the back."

Jonathan agreed with her assessment, but Lucien hadn't been known for his modesty.

"Why don't you check on Hazel and Pete? They should be heading back soon. They'll want to see you."

Guilt wracked his heart now that things had settled. Why hadn't he been here sooner to protect them?

CHAPTER THIRTY

After the incident in the classroom, Hazel tried to comfort the children before walking them home individually. To be honest, she was still shaken from the perilous event herself.

"How are you doing, Peter?" she asked with an arm over his thin shoulders.

"I'm all right. That sort of thing happens a lot around here." He shrugged nonchalantly and kicked a pebble with his booted toe. But no matter his show of courage, streaks of tears stained his cheeks.

"Surely, you haven't been on the receiving end of such an encounter, though."

"No...But I'm all right. Honest. I'm just glad Jon showed up."

"Me, too." She squeezed him closer as they arrived back home to find Jonathan waiting for them outside.

"How are you doing?" Jonathan pulled them in for a bear hug. Having him holding her broke the dam inside, and tears burst from her.

"Hey...it's okay. You're safe now, love." She felt him tug her nearer, and Peter's arms wrapped around her legs holding just as tightly. "Come on, let's go inside."

It took a quarter of an hour for them to settle in the sitting room with a tray of chamomile tea. With her composure reset,

Hazel asked, "What happens now? The Cobblewallers lost their leader. Will they retaliate?"

"No, Lucien was feared more than liked. I'm sure we did a favor for whoever's been wanting to take his spot," Jonathan said as his hand stroked her cheek while another held a cup of tea to her lips.

"Who will that be, I wonder?" she asked after taking a sip.

"It's not for us to worry about. Despite the way it happened, I'm glad to be free of him."

She shuddered, remembering the shock of seeing Lucien and subsequently shooting him before hearing the gunshot that killed him. "Me, too. However horrible that may sound. He's been trying to control you for too long."

The only silver lining to come from the event was her ability to conquer the onset of an attack. She'd held herself together, didn't fall to pieces, and the action buoyed her otherwise lagging spirits.

They spent the rest of the afternoon and early evening together as a family before Hazel retired early, praying a good night's sleep would wash away the stress of the day. Lying in bed, she heard Jonathan come in later then the sound of running water coming from the water closet as he cleaned up. It didn't take long before he joined her in bed and wrapped an arm around her waist.

"I almost lost you today," he whispered behind her ear. "When Mrs. Wilson told me Lucien was here..." A shiver ran through him, and she cuddled deeper into him. "I've never been so terrified in my life, sunshine. And it was all my fault."

"You couldn't have known he'd strike today. At least now we don't have to worry about him any longer."

"I shouldn't have let you and Pete remain here. You should've been safe in a home outside Devil's Haven," he said.

"Nonsense. I can't teach if I'm not here." Stroking his arm, she kissed the warm skin beneath her. "Quit blaming yourself. Wasn't it you who told me it does no good? Or should I revert to guilt over the carriage accident?"

"That's different. I brought this upon our family. And you don't want to be a teacher. You fought it tooth and —"

"Before Lucien interrupted today, I had an epiphany. I realized how ridiculous I've been about the whole thing. If I'm good at it and enjoy teaching, why must it be a consolation prize? My writing isn't going anywhere, and it's true purpose is to educate and entertain children. Even though I forgot that while caught up in what it meant for me." She tangled her fingers with his. "Teaching allows me the same benefits. I just couldn't see it before."

"I'm happy to hear that, but we're still moving and possibly hiring guards to watch over you and the children."

"Like the one you had watching for my return after the holiday?"

"Would you mind?" He propped himself on his elbow to look down at her face, curiosity clear in his expression.

"Not really, as long as he didn't hinder my comings and goings."

"He will if you're heading into danger. I can't risk your safety again after all these attacks." His emerald gaze studied hers. "You truly don't regret tying yourself to a rogue like me even after getting you tangled up in today's mess?"

"Oh, Jonathan..." Taking a leap of faith, she voiced the words she'd been keeping secret for months now. "I love you —

fully and with no regrets. You've believed in me all along, and I have no idea why. You've never tried to hinder my progress, only offered to aid me in further growing. And I realize you may not feel the same —"

He placed a hand over her mouth. "I'm going to stop you right there, sunshine. You are my light, my life." His head dropped as he released a low sigh. "I couldn't say it before because I was a coward, but I'm saying it now because I don't want you to go another day not knowing how much I adore you." Glancing up, he grinned, "I love you, Hazel Travers."

Tears ran down her cheeks as she rolled over to face him fully. Cupping his bearded cheek, she returned his smile. "You're not a coward. And I did have hope that you felt the same. How could I not when you showed me every day — whether it was offering me the classroom as a safe haven from the street or getting the blackboards for the children. You're a kind-hearted man, full of love to give, even if you couldn't voice it until now."

She peppered light kisses over his face.

"I'm not kind."

A watery laugh bubbled up at his denial. "I know it's difficult to believe, but trust me on this. I know my husband, and the man I married is sweet and gentle and..."

He shut her up with a hard kiss to her mouth, his hand tangling in her hair. Breaking away with a gasp, Hazel said, "Don't think to distract me. I love you and want you to believe me when..."

He cut her off again, but this time with a question, vulnerability clear in his tone as he asked her to repeat the sentiment. "You love me?"

"Yes. I, Hazel Travers, love you, Jonathan Travers."

He groaned before letting more of his weight rest on her and kissing her cheeks. "Keep saying that."

So, she did. She told him she loved him as he nibbled his way down her neck. She said it when he nipped at her beaded nipples and when he sought lower treasure, burying his tongue between her folds. And when he thrust his hardened cock inside her, she moaned the words, repeating the litany until they both peaked, replete in their love and satisfaction.

EPILOGUE ONE

"That's all we have time for today. I'll see everyone tomorrow!" Hazel took a seat behind her desk as the children put away their slates and filed out of the room. She couldn't believe how much the class had grown since they'd officially started accepting students. They'd doubled their size, and she'd added on extra class time to manage.

But it was worth it. Seeing the light of knowledge and accomplishment glow on their faces made her feel proud, and she wondered if this was how her father felt as a professor.

"How was class today?" Jonathan entered the emptied room, reaching her desk and leaning over to give her a quick kiss. They'd officially been married six months, and she couldn't be happier. Despite their scandalous beginning, love had grown and was in full bloom now. She couldn't imagine being married to anyone else.

"Interesting as usual. Paul wouldn't stop tugging on Lizzie's braid, so there were some behavioral issues, but nothing I couldn't handle. And today we learned about Shakespeare," she said.

Jonathan's eyebrows lifted in surprise. "Shakespeare? At their age? Most of them can't be more than twelve."

"It's never too early to start studying the Bard."

"I'll take your word for it."

"Were you able to fix Mrs. Robert's squeaky hinge?" she asked, changing the subject. After Jonathan secured the proper permits and deemed the building ready, tenants had moved in at a rapid speed. They even had a waiting list in case of openings. News of safe, affordable housing in Devil's Haven traveled quickly making sure they never lacked residents.

"Yes, though why it squeaked in the first place is beyond me. I only installed it two months ago."

"Well, you better get used to it because as a landlord, it's your responsibility to maintain the upkeep of this place now that you've fixed it."

"Yes, Mrs. Travers, I understand my duties," he said wryly. Coming around the desk, he tugged her up into his arms where he looped them loosely around her back. "And speaking of duties..."

He nibbled at her mouth until she opened for his tongue to sweep in — the taste of mint jolting through her. Moaning, she clutched the front of his jacket, arching into his embrace.

To think, in less than a year, she'd left Hampshire determined to prove herself worthy of living only to discover that she already held value, finding purpose and passion with Jonathan's help.

Now, if only all of her sisters could find the same thing...

EPILOGUE TWO

THREE YEARS LATER

BUBBLES MELTED ON HIS face as Hazel playfully blew them from the palm of her hand. Eyes closed, he warned, "Don't start something you can't finish."

They shared the large clawfoot tub full of hot water and lavender scented oil, Hazel's favorite, as bubbles overflowed from her zealous dose of soap. He relished the slide of her wet body against his and arousal brought his cock to attention.

Wrapping slender arms around his neck, she traced kisses up his neck and hummed. "You should know by now, dear husband, I always accomplish what I set my mind to."

He couldn't deny that particular truth. Although striking out in the beginning of her writing journey, she kept writing and improving until a printer in America agreed to publish her book. Apparently, they saw the value in a story for children that their British counterparts did not.

Searching hands drifted lower until she gripped him and moved with languid strokes, her tongue tracing the line of his jaw. "Did I ever tell you I imagined this once? This exact scene."

"Hmm...really? When was this?" Her husky whisper heated his ear as her teeth nipped the lobe causing him to jerk in response. A low growl rose in his chest at the teasing bite.

"After that first week of seeing you in the rookery. I came home one afternoon once you'd finished your reading, filled the tub, and dreamed of you with me."

"Naughty man...I was a virgin!"

"Made it all the more enticing, love. Thinking of stealing your innocence." He brought his hands to her thighs and maneuvered her body until she sat astride him. "Teaching you what I like."

Shifting his member to her core, Hazel enveloped him in her heat, sinking down on his full length. "Didn't I say you had headmaster tendencies?" Her lips prevented a reply as their mouths mimicked the motion of their bodies. Water sloshed over the tub and splashed to the tile, but neither of them cared.

Jonathan marveled again at his good fortune of having such a passionate, kind, and loving wife. And over the past years of their marriage, their bond only deepened. Thinking of the man he'd been back then — someone trapped in a dangerous, thankless job who felt like he'd never complete what he'd set out to do — he thanked the heavens that they'd seen fit to gift him Hazel.

Their pace quickened, and he heard her breathing change indicating her imminent peak. Reaching below the water, he slid his fingers over her clitoris, circling it the way he knew she liked. "Better hurry, sunshine. I'm hungry for a taste of your quim and liable to take this to the bed before you've finished."

That sent her over the edge. His dirty talk always did. Hazel loved words, especially the downright filthy ones he used during lovemaking. Swallowing her cry of pleasure, he followed her into oblivion, pleased with himself.

His imagination proved no match for the real, flesh and blood Hazel — his love, his wife.

His sunshine.

THE END

THANK YOU FOR READING!

Please consider leaving a rating/review on Amazon and/or Goodreads. Ratings & reviews are the #1 way to support an indie author like me.

They don't have to be long or even positive (though I hope you enjoyed this book!). All the Amazon/Goodreads algorithms care about are QUANTITY.

The more reviews, the more Amazon/Goodreads show my books to other potential readers!

And they serve as guides to readers on whether or not to take a chance on an indie author.

I appreciate your support!

Happy Reading,

Jemma

ABOUT THE AUTHOR

Jemma Frost grew up in the Midwest where she visited the library every day and read romance novels voraciously! Now, she lives in North Carolina with her cat, Spencer, and dreams of stories to be written!

Follow Jemma Frost on Instagram and/or Facebook: @authorjemmafrost

CPSIA information can be obtained
at www.ICGtesting.com
Printed in the USA
LVHW102252161022
730835LV00019B/340